COMMA KAZE

NERD LOVE #1

MELLANIE SZERETO

Comma Kaze

Published by Amatoria Press
Cover art by Amatoria Press

ISBN-13: 978-1-942522-60-7

BOOKS BY MELLANIE SZERETO

The Homegrown Café Book Club series ~
Makin' Bacon
The Farmer Takes a Husband
The Butcher and the Baker
When Harry Met Wally
And Baby Makes 2½
The Homegrown Café Book Club print edition
Love on the Menu series ~
Love Served Hot
Red Hot Pepper
Hot Tamale Nights (2024)
Love on the Menu...Extra Hot standalones ~
Just Desserts
Iced Latté
A Little Appetizer
The Main Dish
Dressing on the Side
Flavor of the Day
Love on the Menu…Steamed trilogy ~
Egging Her On
Sweetening Her Up
Reeling Her In
Love on the Menu: Steam print edition
Nerds & Babies series ~
The Nerd Next Door
The Nerd Upstairs
The Nerd Downstairs (2024)
Nerd Love series ~
Comma Kaze
Comma Sutra (2024)
Comma Con (2025)
Comma Chameleon (2025)

Romancing the Phone series ~
Call Me…Maybe
Smooth Operator
Hang-Ups (2024)
Telephone Lines (2024)
Dialed Up (2025)
Mixed Messages (2025)
The Jerk series ~
Jerk in the Box
Jerk of All Trades
Small Town Jerk
Jerk the Ripper
Two Forks Hollow Christmas short story series ~
Snowballed
Two Nights Before Christmas
Mistletoe Miscalculation (2024)
Standalone Novellas & Short Stories ~
Death Benefits ~ paranormal romance
Mad About You ~ romantic suspense
Behind the Mask ~ contemporary romance
Frostbite ~ contemporary holiday romcom
You Had Me at Goodbye ~ contemporary romcom
Kiss My Sass ~ contemporary romcom
Divorce Actually ~ contemporary romcom
Not Quite Cupid ~ contemporary romcom
Diner 49er ~ contemporary romcom
With Bells On ~ contemporary romcom
G Makes the Spot ~ contemporary romcom
Karma-lized ~ contemporary romcom (2024)
Sexy Claus ~ contemporary holiday romcom (2024)
The Sextet Anthologies ~
Volume 1: Sharing
Volume 2: Dirty Dancing
Volume 3: Occupational Hazards
Volume 4: Entanglements

Volume 5: Mistletoe & Ménage
The Sextet Presents standalones ~
Playing in the Raine: A Toy Story
Bound by Voodoo: Legends
Bewitching Desires series ~
Two if by Sea
Two Knights of Passion
Two Fated for One
Two Pirates to Treasure
Two Times the Trouble
Two Roped and Ready
Two from the Triangle
Beyond Bewitching

CHAPTER ONE

Elijah Clayton lifted the steaming mug to his mouth and pretended to take a drink of his caffè latte, despite the awful stench assaulting his nasal passages. Caffeine wouldn't give him the confidence or the courage he needed. Not even a new suit and tie had nudged him in that direction.

This is stupid. I should just go home and—

"Welcome." A woman with blood-red lipstick offered her hand and a too-white smile. The clipboard tucked under her left arm triggered a cold sweat across the back of his neck. "Let's get you checked in for the interviews. Name?"

He toyed with the idea of saying he wasn't registered for anything, but that wasn't an option—not if he intended to keep his promise. "Um, Elijah. Elijah-34. I mean Elijah M. Clayton, Jr."

After a brisk shake of his hand, the woman ran her finger along the spreadsheet secured under the clip. The tap of her polished nail near the bottom of the page made his stomach twist. "Here's your packet. Place your name tag on the left side of your jacket, where it's visible. The notecards are for interview questions and notes, and please review the rules page. The candidates are listed at the top with first names only and age as they were on the website. Pen?"

He swallowed past the parched desert in his throat as he took the packet she handed him. "No thanks. I have one."

"Excellent. Your first interview is at table nine." She pointed toward the far end of the coffee house slash indie bookstore's meeting space. "Then you'll move down to table ten, up to this end to table one, and so on. The timer will be set for six minutes. At the end of the interviews, we'll have some mix-and-mingle time for those who think they've found potential candidates. Good luck!"

As she turned toward a new arrival, Eli set his mug on the long bar and forced a calming breath.

I can do this. I have *to do this.*

The clock was ticking, and too soon it would stop.

He peeled the paper from the name tag as he reviewed the rules. With limited time at each table, he had to make his questions—and answers—count. Hopefully, his practical nature would serve him well. He positioned the preprinted label with his first name and age on his jacket, careful to align it within the edges of the lapel.

Voices carried from beyond the room, scrambling what little supper he'd eaten, and the hostess gestured for the group to enter.

This is it.

A line of professionally dressed women walked single file through the wide doorway and straight for the row of tables. An invisible cloud of estrogen followed them, permeating the room and settling in his lungs.

Stay focused. Inhale. Exhale.

The man next to him let out a low whistle and leaned closer. "*Damn.* We hit the jackpot tonight. You ever been to one of these before?"

Grateful for the grammatical distraction, Eli shook his head and grabbed his coffee. A sip or two couldn't hurt, could it?

With the first taste, a shudder rippled through him as he fought his gag reflex. He grabbed for a cocktail napkin and covered his mouth, struggling to maintain control of his body.

"Hey, you all right, buddy?"

Embarrassment warmed his cheeks, but Eli nodded and faked a

cough. "Are—" *Rule number four. Don't correct people's grammar unnecessarily.* "Went…down the wrong…ahem…way."

The man snickered. "I don't blame you for choking. Did you see the legs on the blonde in the red skirt? I wouldn't mind going home to that every night."

At a loss for how to respond, Eli patted his pants pockets in search of his keys. The chance to escape proved temptation enough to make him abandon his plan—at least in this context—and forfeit the registration fee. How far was the closest exit?

"May I have your attention please?" The woman with the clipboard now stood near the center of the room with a microphone. "Welcome, ladies and gentlemen. Professionals' Assisted Introductions to Dating thanks you for joining us this evening. I know you're anxious to begin the interviews, so, gentlemen, please go to the first table you've been assigned to. The timer will start as soon as everyone finds their seats."

PAID. Suitable acronym. And it should be "to which you've been assigned."

Eli willed his legs to carry him to table nine. The reminder of how much he'd doled out to participate in this civilized version of speed dating was sufficient incentive to make the best of the situation. Leaving now would only draw attention to him and the worst that could happen was he wouldn't meet his future wife.

He unbuttoned his suit coat as he sat across from the first potential Mrs. Clayton—the blonde woman in the red skirt.

A hiss of static from the microphone brought his attention back to the clipboard lady. "The timer will sound in exactly six minutes. Gentlemen, please move to the next interview at that time. Begin!"

A business card snapped against the table with the help of long, tapered fingers. "Hi, I'm Mandy Hunt, a junior partner at Edmunds, Galway, and Updike. I specialize in high-profile divorce cases."

He pulled a business card from the inside pocket of his jacket and handed it to her. "Elijah Clayton. I'm an English professor and a poet." *Mandy. Thirty-five years old. Remember the questions.* "Do you want to have children when you get married?"

She wrinkled her nose and frowned. "No. Nearly forty percent of marriages end in divorce. Why would I subject a child to that?"

Well, that was quick. One down, nine to go. "I—"

"I suppose you have some deep-seated desire to have your name passed on to the next generation?" Her accusatory tone hit a raw nerve.

"No, I think family is important." Done with the conversation, he retrieved a note card and his pen. *#9. Mandy-35 Kids? No.*

After several awkward minutes of her fingertips galloping on the table, a bell sounded and he moved to table ten with no regrets.

As he settled across from a tall redheaded woman with Zoe typed on her name tag, she grimaced and removed her cell phone from her hip pocket. "Sorry, um…" She grasped his lapel. "Elijah. One of my patients just arrived at the hospital and her contractions are three minutes apart. I have to go."

A second later, she was gone. He added another comment to his notes, this time with more creativity.

Zoe-34. Hmm. I'm at table ten…with no one to interview…as possible wife. Her occupation…interferes with my notion…of family life.

At least this particular six minutes of his life hadn't been a complete waste of time. His students would enjoy a nontraditional example of a two-part haiku with a twist of rhyme, although they didn't need to know it was about his personal life.

He reread the poem several times before coming to the conclusion that few in his classes would mistake the experience as someone else's.

The bell sounded again, sending him to the opposite end of the room. A brunette with glasses waited for him at table one, her hands clutched in her lap and a deer-in-headlights look in her eyes. Maybe she was as uncomfortable as he was.

"Hi, I'm Elijah." He slid the chair closer to the table and sat.

"I'm Beatrix." Her angelic voice instantly soothed his nerves. "Tell me about yourself."

Beatrix. Thirty-five. "I write poetry. Oh, and I'm an English professor." Relaxing into the seat, he shuffled through his mental list of questions. "I want to get married. Soon. Do you like kids?"

A pretty blush spread across her cheeks. "Yeah. I have lots of nieces and nephews. I'm a songwriter in my free time. What kind of poetry do you write?"

"Wow, a songwriter? What instruments do you play? Do you sing too? You have a nice voice." *I found her. I might have actually found her.* "I prefer sonnets and free verse, but I can come up with a decent haiku or limerick on occasion."

"Guitar, piano, and flute. Yes, I sing. Limericks are fun." She smiled, genuine pleasure seeming to shine in her eyes.

The questions. I have to ask the questions. "How do you feel about breastfeeding? I think it's important for babies to have the health advantages of nursing, plus the bonding time."

The color drained from her lips as she pressed them into a rigid line. "I think breastfeeding is best, if it's an option."

Was that question too personal?

She straightened in her chair and exhaled. "Do you have a big family? Brothers and sisters and cousins?"

An all-too-familiar pang spread through his chest. "I'm an only child and my parents live in Colorado where I grew up. My cousin is like a sister. She's the reason I accepted the job offer here."

"I have three sisters and two brothers. How long have you been in Ohio?"

"Akron area since August, but I was in Columbus for my Master's before I went back to Colorado for my PhD. Then I lived in Missouri for my first job. I'm tired of moving around, so I'd like to stay here."

She leaned forward and lowered her voice. "What do you think about going for a walk after this is over?"

The tension in his shoulders and neck eased for the first time in weeks, but the ring of the bell stole his chance to enjoy it. Six minutes hadn't passed half as quickly with the divorce lawyer. He nodded instead of grabbing Beatrix's arm and dragging her to the exit. "That sounds great. I'll meet you back here in…forty-two minutes."

She smiled again, sparking a strange hiccup in his pulse. "See you then."

With his heart thumping and his feet barely touching the ground, he floated to the next stop. Thankfully, the dark-haired CPA seemed more interested in managing his retirement plan than finding out if he'd make a good husband.

Thirty-five minutes and six more introductions later, the seconds on his watch ticked away far too slowly. The interior designer across from him glanced to the left and back again, either following his straying eyes or looking for one of her earlier interviewees.

She rose almost as fast as he did when the final bell tolled. "Good to meet you, Elijah. Best of luck."

A man in a blue suit met her halfway around the table, but Eli didn't stay to find out if they'd connected the way he and Beatrix had. He hurried through the noisy group moving toward him. After stressing over this aspect of his life since shortly after his permanent cross-country move, a solution was finally within reach.

I can keep my promise.

As he finally cleared the last couple, Beatrix stood, looping her purse strap over her head and across her body. He resisted placing his palm against his belly to calm the sudden horde of unruly dragons. It wouldn't help anyway. Only years of self-discipline stopped him from taking the easy way out—the quickest route home.

She looked his direction and waved. She hadn't rushed out the door at the first opportunity, unlike the woman he'd met at a conference icebreaker last month.

I must've done something right for a change.

Or he'd gotten really lucky.

"Hi, Elijah. Are you ready to go?" Her melodic voice urged him to follow her wherever she led. "There's a quiet little tea room on the next block."

"Ready. I've been there a few times." He walked beside her to the doorway and nearly jumped out of his skin when she tucked her hand into the bend of his left elbow. *Conversation. Talk to her. And don't be boring.* "Um, I don't drink coffee, but I like tea. They have a good selection of herbal and rooibos teas. Caffeine makes me edgy, so I avoid it."

"Does talking to women make you edgy?" Without slowing, she guided him through the large revolving door leading to the sidewalk.

"No." The slight chill from the early October evening cooled the warmth on his cheeks from the half-truth. The deadline that was closing in too fast messed with his mind more than interacting with the opposite sex. After a couple slow breaths, his mental list of questions came back into focus. "You have experience with babies?"

"Mm-hm. All but one of my brothers and sisters are married with kids—five nieces and three nephews—so I babysit a lot. My youngest sister is due with her first next week. Another girl." She glanced sideways at him as they reached the entrance to the tea room, but she didn't hesitate when he held the door for her. "You know, men usually run the other direction at the mention of babies, especially before the first date."

Unsure if she expected an explanation of his interest, he shrugged. Telling her the whole story had to wait until he was sure she would make a suitable wife and mother. "We all started out as babies. They're just small humans. How do you feel about adoption?"

She paused mid-step and stared at him for a full three seconds, sending his stomach whirling for the umpteenth time. "I could love a child who doesn't share my genes just as much as one who does. Mother doesn't have to be a biological term."

She's perfect. Don't screw this up. "Should I pay for your tea? Or would you rather we each buy our own this time?"

"Do you expect anything in return if you buy?" Her serious tone caught him off guard.

Does she mean I think she should pay next time? "No." He stepped toward the cashier at the counter. "I'd like a medium amaretto rooibos."

Beatrix cast another look his direction. "I'll have the same."

Not even attempting to decipher her confusing pout, he handed the cashier enough cash to cover both drinks and a reasonable tip. "Keep the change."

As the barista prepared their tea, his most-promising prospect gestured toward the seating area. "I'll grab a table. That was nice, by the way. Most people don't tip at coffee shops."

An upswing to counter the last dip of uncertainty made him wish choosing a wife was as simple as shopping for socks—a hundred-percent-cotton black crew since they matched everything. The social interaction of dating was worse than any rollercoaster he'd ever imagined not riding.

With a cup in each hand, he headed to the table his new potential wife had claimed. Her neutral expression set off yet another strange feeling in his chest. Why couldn't people hold signs that told others exactly how they felt?

Of course, his sign would reveal the anxiety he worked so hard to hide.

She glanced toward the chair beside her, hinting that she wasn't perched on the edge of her seat, ready to run for the exit. "I love the smell of amaretto. It reminds me of these cookies my grandma always makes at Christmastime."

"My cousin always sent me amaretto cookies when I was in college." He bit the inside of his cheek to hold his emotions in check as he sat.

"Are you okay? You seem upset about something." Beatrix removed the lid from her cup and a wisp of steam rose toward her face.

"She's going to die soon." The lettering on the window blurred, but he didn't give in to the urge to vent about the unfairness of life. It wouldn't change anything.

Her warm fingers closed around his. "I'm sorry. You said she's like a sister to you. I can't imagine losing one of my sisters, even if they do get on my nerves sometimes. Cancer?"

He sipped his tea, hoping it would wash down the lump in his throat. It didn't work. "Brain tumor. Late stage. Terminal."

"That's terrible. Can I do anything to help?"

Grateful for an opening to his next question, he faced her. "Maybe. Do you think you could lactate without having a baby?"

"Geez. You probably don't even have a cousin, let alone one that's dying." She jerked her hand away and pushed the chair away from the table, creating an ear-jarring screech. Her mouth opened and closed twice. Then she dug through her purse and tossed several ones at him. “Keep the change, pervert.”

Tea in hand, she hurried out the door.

What had he done wrong this time?

CHAPTER TWO

STILL DISGUSTED WITH LAST NIGHT'S WASTE OF MONEY AND HOPE, Beatrix yanked on a long-sleeved company T-shirt to go with her jeans. Elijah-34 was the final straw in a long line of losers she'd found through the dating services her little sister had insisted she try.

Dying cousin, my ass. What kind of thirty-four-year-old weirdo asks a woman if she'll let him nurse like a baby?

She shoved her feet into her boots and headed to the kitchen to make a fried egg sandwich. Her cell phone buzzed in her hand on her way to the fridge. A few taps on the screen opened her text messages.

"Hey, Trixie! How'd it go last night?"

"You are *so* on my shit list, Shell. You can damn well wait until I've had breakfast for an answer. And that's Aunt Bea to you from now on, missy." She pulled a package of Canadian bacon and another of pepper jack cheese from the meat drawer and set them on the counter. Eggs, butter, and orange juice followed. A few well-timed bangs of pots and pans drowned out the buzzing that continued every few seconds or so. "Sooner or later, you're going to have to make a bathroom run. Your persistence is no match for my stubbornness or your squished bladder."

She dropped two slices of seedless rye in the toaster and turned on the burner to preheat the iron skillet. As she plopped a dab of butter in the pan, her business phone rang.

Gads, I can't catch a stinkin' break this morning.

The egg sizzled and spread through the first of the two rings prior to the answering machine kicking on. She gave the yolk a few stabs with the sharp edge of the eggshell to break it and sprinkled on a dash of salt and a good dose of black pepper. As her message greeting began, she flipped the egg and then topped it with a single piece of Canadian bacon.

"You have reached Glouster Plumbing. Please leave your name and number, and I'll call you back as soon as I can. Business hours are eight to five. After-hours rates may apply to emergency calls. Thanks for your business." The beep sounded far too cheery.

"The bathroom faucet is spraying water everywhere! What do I do? Please call me back before the house floods." He rattled off his number and address while she buttered her toast. The clang of the butter knife in the sink drowned out the next word. "—Clayton. Are you there? Please answer the phone."

Taking pity on the poor inept soul, she grabbed the receiver and wedged it between her ear and her shoulder. "Open the cabinet under the sink. See the valves? Turn both of them all the way to the right. Clockwise. That'll shut off your water until I can get there. You're not very far away, so I should be there in about fifteen minutes or so."

After several moments of mumbles and grunts, breathing sounded in the receiver. "I think I turned the right valve things. Why did the faucet handle break off? Aren't they made of metal? How am I ever going to clean up this mess?"

She added a slice of cheese and the contents of the skillet to her sandwich. "Calm down. We'll figure it out. For now, throw some towels on the floor to keep the water from soaking through the flooring. Replacing a rotted floor is a whole lot more expensive than a new faucet. Be sure to wipe down the cabinet too. Inside and out. I'll be there as quick as I can."

"Okay. Towels on the floor and dry the cabinet." A pathetic sigh carried through the phone. "I'm going to be late for work, aren't I?"

Hmm, computer geek or numbers nerd? "Looks that way, but I should have you ready to go in less than an hour if I don't run into any surprises."

"I don't like surprises."

Neither do I, buddy. "Unless you have a bad connection, it should be an easy fix. I'll be there by seven."

"Okay." He sighed into the phone. "Would you mind coming to the patio doors farthest from the garage at the back of the house? I don't want to track water through the house."

"Sure. Be there shortly, Mr. Clayton." She hung up before her first gig of the day talked her into helping him with cleanup too.

Then again, sucking who knew how many gallons of water from his bathroom floor would delay the job at her older sister Maddie's house. By now, Shelley had probably blabbed to all of their siblings about last night's attempt to meet educated, well-mannered men who weren't skittish about babies or determined to produce their own offspring.

In the interest of more word-of-mouth recommendations, Beatrix wrapped her sandwich in a napkin, filled her travel mug with orange juice, and pocketed her cell phone. On her way out the door, she plucked her keys from the hook.

The earlier-than-usual start of her day meant less traffic, improving her mood enough to consider offering the use of her wet-dry vac. She even arrived at her destination five minutes ahead of her estimate. After a last gulp of juice to wash down her breakfast, she checked her teeth in the rearview mirror. *All clear.*

Stepping stones led her along the side of the garage toward the backyard. As she rounded the corner, her cell vibrated against her hip. Without reading the latest text in the lengthy string of one-sided conversation, she tapped in the only answer she could. "*Emergency plumbing job, Shell. Later.*"

A deck with built-in benches and a covered grill stretched the length of the house. Impressed by the design, she almost stopped to take snap a picture. *Work first.*

The closest set of doors seemed to lead into a family room, so she continued to the second set. *Kitchen. On to the last one.* It was open about a foot, revealing a guy wearing a white T-shirt and boxer briefs. He was on his hands and knees on the far side of what seemed to be a master bedroom.

She rapped her knuckles on the glass. “Hello? Mr. Clayton? Trixie Glouster from Glouster Plumbing.”

Water dripped from somewhere above him and landed in his rumpled dark hair. The man rubbed his sleeve along his forehead without so much as a glance in her direction. His bicep flexed with the movement. “I keep wiping, but the floor’s still wet. And the ceiling. I ran out of dry towels because I’m behind on laundry and I haven’t even started drying the cabinet.”

“Not a problem. I carry lots of shop towels in my truck.”

Two steps into the bedroom gave her a clear view of tan carpet at least two shades darker at the bathroom doorway and a trail of footprints toward the bed and back. Her newest client’s clothes clung to his skin, also hinting at the amount of water that had escaped the faucet before he’d managed to call her and turn off the tap.

The urge to take care of him hit with the usual super-strength idiocy that helpless men inspired. She dug her key ring from her pocket and jabbed her truck key into her palm to curb the stupid impulse. “I’ll be back in a minute with the towels. Do you have a GFCI outlet where I can plug in a Shop-Vac?”

“GFCI?”

Good God, it’s a wonder he hasn’t electrocuted himself. “The kind that automatically shuts off when it’s exposed to water. It has a red reset button in the center.”

“I think there’s one on the deck.” He made another pass over the tile and sighed. “Are you sure you can fix this?”

“Yep. Back in a few seconds.” Leaving him to his hopeless task, she stepped back outside and scuttled down the steps.

Just call me the fix-it queen. How did she always manage to end up playing mother to everybody?

The drenched state of the man and his floor mandated balancing an entire duffle bag of clean towels on one shoulder and toting the vacuum with her free hand. A quick scan of the back wall of the house yielded a suitable outlet outside the patio doors.

She set the vac on the deck and walked into the bedroom. Half a minute later, she tossed three towels toward Clayton's drenched backside. "Spread those on the floor while I get the rest of my stuff."

By the time she returned with her bucket of wrenches, screwdrivers, and assorted plumbing supplies, he stood at the edge of the carpet, the wet T-shirt clinging to his toned but not bulging back muscles. The tight butt below it was every bit as perfect.

She swallowed an appreciative hum. "I brought in a few faucet styles to choose from. A couple are four-inch centers and—" The face that appeared as he turned sparked her temper. "You. I don't believe this. Elijah-34. The pervert."

"Wait a minute." He frowned as he wrung the fingers of his left hand with his right and then repeated the action with his other hand. "Your name is Beatrix, not Trixie. And you're a songwriter, not a plumber. Where are your glasses?"

"Ever heard of contact lenses? And men I meet in social situations tend to take me more seriously when I go by Beatrix." *The perv? Or my family? Which is the lesser of two evils?*

"Trixie is a nice name." His frown deepened. "I'm not a pervert."

She snorted. "What do you call yourself then? A fetishist?"

A flood of pink colored his cheeks. "I don't have any…fetishes. Can you just fix my sink? I need to go to work."

"Fine." Aggravated by his denial, she plunked the faucet selections on the bed. "Pick one and then stay out of my way."

"The one on this end." He took two steps toward what was probably a closet and stopped, like he suddenly realized he'd left more damp footprints on the carpet. His hands gripped the hem of his T-shirt. "Turn around. I need to get dressed."

"Oh, please. I have two brothers. It's not like I've never seen a guy without a shirt before." She picked up the style he'd indicated and marched to the bathroom. "Or naked, for that matter. By the way, undressed comes first, unless you plan on wearing wet undies."

A sound somewhere between a whimper and a choke came from behind her.

Snickering at his reaction, she focused her attention on disconnecting the broken faucet. One look at the handle sent her into the bedroom again. "You can't replace a two-handle faucet with a single—"

Bare ass cheeks greeted her when she looked up from the box.

Elijah spun around, giving her a full-frontal view. "What are you *doing*?"

The horror in his voice did little to distract her from staring at his most satisfactory equipment. "Enjoying the scenery."

His dick bobbed and stiffened enough to point straight at her. Color bloomed across his neck and face again. "Stop looking!"

"Would you rather I touch?" Certain he'd balk at her confrontational tone, she walked toward him with her hand outstretched.

"Yes. I mean no!" He grabbed for the wet boxers at his feet and jerked them on. "You're taunting me, aren't you?"

She bit her lip to stem the twinge of guilt and shrugged. After all, he was right. She'd had high hopes that she might have finally met a nice, good-looking guy with brains last night. He deserved a little retaliation.

"That's what I thought." He shook his head and picked up his wallet from the dresser. "How much do I owe you for the service call?"

"You're *firing* me?" Outrage wrestled with remorse and the desire to maintain her spotless satisfaction rating. "Look, I'm sorry. It was unprofessional of me to take out my…pissed-off-ness on you. I can be done replacing the faucet in ten minutes and I'll throw in the wet vac and wipe down at no extra charge."

"Pissed-off-ness? That isn't a word." His pained look warned her the apology could've been better. "Okay, but only because I don't have time to call someone else."

A curt nod was the best she could manage. She swapped the box for the correct one, grabbed a few more towels, and walked to the bathroom without a backward glance.

Three frustration-powered tugs on the wrench loosened the first connection beneath the sink, sending a spray of ice-cold water at her chest. "Holy frozen waterfalls!"

Boisterous laughter drowned out her self-recriminations for not draining the intact line before she disconnected it.

As she stood to flip open the cold-water tap, Elijah appeared in the doorway, dressed in dry boxer briefs and an undershirt. "Your shirt is wet."

"No kidding." Too peeved at him to be concerned about a negative review, she yanked her shirt off and tossed it to him. "Oops. Looks like my bra got wet too. I better take it off."

As she unsnapped the front closure, his hands closed over the thin layer of fabric covering her breasts. He moved with her when she tried to step away.

Well, that backfired.

"I'm sorry I laughed! I couldn't help it. I didn't mean to…"

His palms rubbed against her taut nipples, triggering a zip of pleasure between her thighs. She barely suppressed a moan. "Unless you plan to finish what you started, you need to let go right now."

Without releasing her, he looked down, obviously noticing the erection that strained to reach her naked skin. "I… You… I've never… I didn't…"

Unable to resist, she took a step closer. His cock twitched against her and left a trail of fire near her belly button. "I guess that means you're not stopping."

He pulled his hands away, snagging his watch on the lace and yanking the right cup from her breast. His eyes widened and his heavy breathing changed to shallow panting, but he didn't retreat. The other cup slipped free as his flailing succeeded in unsnagging his watch. "N—no? I mean yes. Um… Not stopping?"

She tugged his T-shirt up to his underarms and pressed her achy nipples to his chest. The smattering of dark hair against her skin coaxed out a groan. "Then kiss me."

The tentative touch of his lips on hers spoke of a man who was either an expert tease or had little sexual experience. She nipped at his lower lip and slid her tongue into his mouth when he gasped.

He deepened the kiss, his suddenly aggressive move setting off a geyser of desire through her veins. Grasping her hips, he pushed his erection against her belly and rocked forward. The thin cotton of his boxers did little to disguise his fully erect length and girth.

Guiding him backward, she walked toward the bed, intent on turning their chemistry into something more explosive than verbal sparring. She shoved his boxers down a moment before the backs of his legs hit the mattress. After a final sweep along his molars, she broke the kiss and used a firm hand to his chest to send him flat on his back onto the bed. “Condoms in the nightstand?”

His slow nod brought a surge of relief. She always went out prepared, but a plumbing job had never included an inspection of this type.

A quick search of the drawer produced two unopened boxes. She removed one foil packet and tossed it to him. “Put it on.”

He looked toward the packet near his arm as she toed off her boots and worked on unfastening her jeans. Second thoughts stood out all over his face, from his glassy eyes to his trembling jaw.

What the h—

A burst of classical music made them both jump.

He scurried across the bed with his boxers around his knees and his ass in the air to grab his cell phone from the other nightstand. “I have to answer this.”

Her attempt not to roll her eyes failed. “Of course you do.”

With his phone to his ear, he sat facing away from her. “Chloe, I’m here. Is everything okay?”

Chloe? Beatrix leaned her head back and focused her attention on the smooth white ceiling. *Wife? Girlfriend?*

An almost inaudible squeak came from across the bed. “I’ll be there in…ten minutes. Wait for me, okay?”

The agony in his voice forced her to look at him. His shoulders slumped forward and he rested his face in his palms. The cheating SOB obviously felt guilty about something.

She refastened her jeans and sat on the floor to put on her boots. “You’re going to have to call another plumber. I—”

“It’s time.” A sob broke a long moment of silence. Another followed.

Scrambling to her feet, she tried to stop the overwhelming impulse to comfort him, but nothing ever worked against tears. Bra re-hooked and T-shirt in place, she rounded the end of the bed. “Are you okay?”

His nod failed to convince her. Then he glanced up at her with ashen skin and an anguished expression. “It’s time.”

“Time for what? What happened?”

He dropped his chin to his chest. “Time for Chloe to die.”

Oh shit, the cousin is real.

CHAPTER THREE

SEVEN WEEKS OF KNOWING CHLOE WOULD DIE HADN'T PREPARED ELI for the onslaught of grief brought on by his cousin's call. Every cell in his body ached from the knowledge that she wouldn't survive more than a few days. His promise loomed over him with new gravity.

I'm not ready. I can't do this.

He pressed the heels of his hands to his eyelids for several seconds, hoping to stop the sting of tears.

I have to. I told her I would.

Determined to pull himself together, he took a slow breath as he stood. The room wobbled and swayed. "I have to hurry."

Beatrix grabbed his arm. "Sit. You look like you're going to pass out."

"Let go." He batted at the hand on his shoulder, panic setting in with the realization that at least a full minute had passed since he promised to be at the hospital in ten minutes. "I have to get dressed. I have to leave."

"Sit, damn it." Her firm tone warned him to follow her directions or suffer the consequences. She dug a pair of pants, a shirt, and socks from the hamper and tossed them at him. "Get dressed. I'll drive you—but only because you're a danger to everybody else on the road."

She dragged her bag of towels toward the bathroom as he slipped on the wrinkled dress pants he'd worn to work yesterday. By the time he slid his arms into the equally rumpled shirt, she'd emptied the entire contents onto the floor and counter. His socks and shoes proved to be the hardest struggle, his balance going haywire whenever he bent over to reach for his feet.

"You ready?" Standing at the end of the bed, she adjusted her ponytail. "Get your phone and your keys. Do you have an extra set? I can come back and fix the faucet and clean up after I drop you off."

A tightening in his chest caught him off guard. "You're not staying with me?"

Her sigh probably meant something, but he had no idea what. "We'll see. Now let's go before I change my mind."

Her hand closed around his, giving him a small measure of comfort, and she led him to the French doors. After rolling her barrel-shaped vacuum inside, she closed and locked the door from the inside. Her brisk pace toward the hallway suggested she didn't need directions to the front door.

"Which hospital?" She glanced to the side as they passed the spare bathroom and again toward the nursery Chloe had helped him set up the day he'd agreed to become her daughter's legal guardian. When Beatrix stopped dead in her tracks half a step past the baby's room, he almost tripped over his own feet. Her low growl sent a shiver up his spine. "You have *got* to be kidding me. If you're married, I may just find a new use for my pipe wrench."

"What did I do now? I'm not married! I'm trying to find a wife." Too overwhelmed by the turn of events to even think about her confusing threat, he continued down the hall. "And people call *me* strange."

Footsteps sounded behind him, but he didn't slow. Time had suddenly accelerated and he had no intention of wasting it.

At the front door, she slammed her palm against the door before he could do more than grab the knob. "We almost had sex. You owe me an explanation."

He willed his racing heart to go back to its normal rhythm at her reminder. "For what? My cousin is dying and I have be with her right now."

She removed her hand and then followed him to her truck. "Fine, but don't think I'm letting you off the hook. I drive. You talk."

Rather than argue with her, he climbed in the passenger seat and buckled his seatbelt. According to everything he'd read about women in preparation for his search, his best option was to apologize and give her flowers. Too bad he had no idea what he'd done wrong.

She started the engine. "You know, maybe you better keep quiet while I'm driving. Tell me where we're going."

To speak or not to speak. That is the question.

Settling on a possible way to avoid contradicting her orders, he tapped the map app on his phone and typed in the name of the hospital. A couple seconds later, detailed directions appeared. He reached across the center console to show her the screen and held his breath.

The narrowed-eyed look she gave him should've singed his eyebrows. She put the truck in gear and backed out of the driveway. Silence reigned for the next seven minutes, even as she entered the parking garage.

He unbuckled as soon as she pulled into a space. "Thanks for the ride. You don't have to—"

"I'm coming in, whether you like it or not. We have some things to discuss."

"I know I did or said something stupid. I do that a lot. But right now, the only thing that matters is Chloe." Hoping she'd drop the subject, he got out of the truck and took the shortest route toward the main entrance.

The clunk of her door closing echoed through the concrete structure. Then the steady *clip-clop* of her boots grew closer.

"Wait up." She grasped his hand, the action so at odds with her behavior that he couldn't ignore the unexpected warmth that crept up his arm. "I'll stay if you want me to."

Was she trying to confuse him on purpose?

Unsure how to respond, he stayed silent until they reached the nurses' station in the cancer wing. He returned the wave of the woman who usually helped Chloe with her sponge bath. Her smile wasn't as wide as it had been yesterday.

Another nurse patted him on the upper arm as she passed him. "G'morning, Mr. Clayton. She's awake and waiting for you."

He bit the inside of his lower lip and tightened his hold on Beatrix's hand. A nod of acknowledgment seemed appropriate, but his neck was too stiff to cooperate. "Thanks."

A quick look in the direction of Chloe's room sparked the urge to run home and hide. Three doctors stood in a tight circle, each one familiar from the last seven weeks of daily visits and updates.

The oncologist motioned for him to join them. "We had difficulty waking Chloe this morning. She was disoriented when the nurse checked her vitals. Her heart rate is up and her blood-oxygen levels are dropping. She has possibly two to four days. Maybe a bit shorter or longer, but soon. It's time to deal with the other part of the equation."

The knot in Eli's throat ached, but his heart hurt more. "I understand. Can I see her?"

"You have about fifteen minutes. Make it count, just in case." The doctor squeezed Eli's shoulder. "You're a good guy, Eli. I wish we could've met under better circumstances."

A nod came easier than words this time, and Eli fought a bout of lightheadedness to get into the room, not wanting to waste the precious seconds he had left with his cousin. Slight resistance slowed him as he entered.

"Do you want me to wait out here?" Beatrix's soft question reminded him of her presence.

How had she become an unnoticed extension of him where they touched?

He shook his head. "You should meet her."

"If you're sure." She walked beside him as they approached the bed. Her faint gasp suggested she'd never seen anyone in the final days of life before.

"Eli." Chloe's dark eyelashes brushed her now-grayish skin in a slow-motion blink. "I'm ready. You are too." Her lips curved into a gentle smile and she looked to his left. "Hi, I'm Chloe. I told Eli he'd find you. You're going to be a wonderful mother."

Beatrix cleared her throat. "I'm Beatrix, but you can call me Trixie. Um, mother? What do you mean?"

He pretended not to notice her sideways glance.

Chloe's fingers flexed where they rested on her distended belly. "You were supposed to tell her."

"Tell me what, Eli?" Beatrix narrowed her eyes at him. They widened a second later. "The questions. You're looking for a wife because… Your cousin… And the baby's room. *Mother?*"

He pinched the bridge of his nose with his free hand. "I *tried* to tell her, Chloe, but I'm just not good at talking to people."

A boot connected with his anklebone, but the pain was negligible compared to that of losing his closest friend. "No kidding."

"Trixie. Eli. You're upsetting Eve." Chloe's eyes drifted closed as she frowned.

Having seen that indication of pain many times over the past several weeks, he reached toward the call button.

Her fingers closed around his wrist and brought his hand to a firm spot low on her belly. "That's her head. She wants to know you're going to take care of her when I'm gone. You too, Trixie. Put your hand next to Eli's."

Every bit of color in Beatrix's cheeks drained from her face. "I can't—"

"Eve needs you, and Eli brought you here. I trust you with the two people who are most important to me."

Beatrix grimaced and touched her fingertips to Eve's head as the baby shifted. She snatched her arm back and tried to tug free from their linked hands. "Let go, Eli. I can't do this."

Well versed in what anxiety could do to a person forced into an uncomfortable situation, he released her. The calming warmth disappeared with her as she rushed out of the room.

He dropped his chin to his chest and swallowed past the lump in his throat. "I'm sorry I failed, Chloe. I'll find a way to raise Eve by myself. I can start teaching online classes or something so I can work from home."

"You didn't fail. Trixie will be there for you and the baby."

Yeah, that's why she ran away. The nonsensical talk the doctor had mentioned as a way to gauge the tumor's progression had evidently started.

A knock on the open door made his pulse jump. Unfortunately, a nurse walked into the room instead of Beatrix. Even to his untrained eye, she wore a fake smile.

"It's time to deliver that sweet baby." She adjusted the blanket over Chloe's abdomen and checked the IV. "Mr. Clayton, are you sure you want to be present during the procedure? It's not too late to change your mind if you're feeling squeamish."

Steeling his nerves against the image of scalpels and blood from the Caesarian video he'd endured, he blew out a slow breath. "I want to be there with Chloe."

"She's darn lucky to have you. Head out to the nurses' station so we can get you into a set of scrubs. As soon as we have Chloe settled in, you can join us to welcome that little one into the world."

Doubt that he'd ever see his cousin alive again crept in and he leaned over the rail to give her a careful hug.

Even as weak as she had to be, she wrapped her arms around him tighter than usual. "I love you, Eli. Forever and ever."

Tears stung his eyes, but he blinked them away. "I love you too, Chloe. Always."

Walking out of the room took enough self-discipline to trigger a surge of pain through his entire body. Only the knowledge that she would die at peace gave him the will to put one foot in front of the other as he walked the length of hallway. He wouldn't let her down, no matter what happened.

Several steps from his destination, a tug on his shirt brought him to a halt, but he didn't have to look over his shoulder to know who stood inches behind him. A mix of grief and determination overpowered his anger. "I thought you left."

"I started to, but I only made it to the elevator. I'm sorry. My issues don't begin to compare to what your cousin is going through." Beatrix let go of his shirt and stepped around him, not quite meeting his gaze. "I also promised to stay with you."

Her apology deflated his irritation and made him wish for a physical connection to her again.

Why does she have to be so confusing? "You don't have to come in during the surgery if you don't want to, but I have to make sure Chloe gets to hold her baby."

"You'll pass out without somebody there to distract you. Are you sure it's okay for me to be there? Where do we need to go?"

"It's what Chloe wants. The doctor promised to make special arrangements for a larger room." Grateful not to be on his own, he resisted an automatic denial that he wouldn't faint. "The nurse told me to come out here to the desk. I need to put on scrubs."

"Okay." Her cool fingers slipped through his, renewing the welcome calm her touch brought. "I'm ready if you are."

Ten minutes later, he fought a wave of dizziness as they waited for the nurse outside the operating room. He closed his eyes and tried to imagine a library with endless shelves filled with thousands and thousands of books, but a picture of Chloe dying before Eve was even born obliterated everything else.

"Elijah, they're ready for us." Beatrix's voice trembled almost as much as his insides, making him curious about her issues.

He focused on the way her smaller hand fit into his. "Are we ready?"

"I think so."

"Okay." A slow inhale and exhale lifted the fog enough for him to take a step through the double doors. He tightened his grip on her hand and focused on walking to the operating table where Chloe lay.

His cousin smiled at him. "Told you so."

For once, he was glad to hear that gentle reprimand. *I hope you're right.* "I should've listened to you more often."

"Yep." Her laugh sounded coarse and she followed it with a cough. "Trixie, thank you for being here."

The obstetrician joined the nurse on the opposite side of the bed.

Her mask and cap hid all but her eyes and a narrow strip of her forehead. "Chloe, I need to know right away if you can feel anything besides some pressure—any pain, sudden disorientation, anything at all. The anesthesiologist is standing by in case we need to put you fully under. Eli and Trixie, you need to be ready to leave the room, just in case we run into complications. I don't foresee any problems, but I like to be prepared. Everybody ready?"

At Chloe's soft reply, the doctor took her place beyond the sheet draped over the lower two-thirds of her patient's body. Eli stood with his back to the delivery team and willed the procedure to go smoothly.

Beatrix's knuckles turned white where she grasped the lowered bed railing. "Eve is a pretty name. Is it special for some reason? Or do you just like it?"

Chloe seemed to stare at a point on the ceiling above them. "My middle name is Evelyn, which is little old fashioned. Brian—my husband—and I decided to call her Eve. Evelyn Brianna. He was so excited. He's waiting for me."

Memories of the day Brian had been laid to rest filled Eli's mind. Chloe's heartache had disguised the symptoms of her illness even then. Every headache and bout of dizziness had been attributed to the pain of losing her husband and bearing their child alone.

A grimace on her previously serene face brought a stab of panic to his chest. "Are you okay?"

"I can't go yet. I have to tell Brian what shee looksh like and how shee feelsh in my armsh."

Slurring. Two to five days.

He shouldn't have searched late-stage symptoms on the internet. Every new change made the prognosis more real, more final.

He clamped his mouth closed to keep from yelling at the doctors to hurry, but it didn't stop the burning sensation in his eyes or the tightness in his chest.

The end was coming, and he couldn't slow its arrival.

CHAPTER FOUR

The vise on Beatrix's hand squeezed tighter, making the numbness mutate into prickles. She didn't dare try to get free, though. If Eli turned his attention to her, he might realize how close she was to leaving—for good. Memories and the overpowering smell of antiseptic threatened to force her breakfast out of her stomach.

Suck it up! A woman is dying, for God's sake.

A vigorous cry came from the other side of the sheet, and a mix of relief, hope, and heartbreak drowned out everything but the desire to see Chloe cradle her child for what could be the only opportunity in their lives.

"Congratulations." The disembodied female voice sounded like one of the women who had greeted her and Eli at the nurses' station. "You have a precious daughter. Ten fingers and ten of the cutest little toes. Give us a minute to clean her up a bit and then she's all yours."

The doctor who'd done the talking when they arrived at the hospital looked from the monitors toward the patient whose vital signs he'd been monitoring. "Great job, Chloe. Any discomfort or pain?"

With half-closed eyelids, Chloe moved her head from side to side. "Jus'sleep…ee."

"That's okay. You're allowed to rest while we take care of you and

Eve." Although he didn't seem to have any immediate concerns, his serious tone left no doubt that the clock was her enemy.

Eli shifted beside Beatrix, his hold loosening slightly. The prickly sensation changed to a heavy ache that matched the feeling in the rest of her body and soul. What should've been a joyous occasion was overshadowed by tragedy and injustice. Why did Chloe have to die?

Hushed voices amplified the funereal mood of the room. Even the baby was quiet as her caretakers completed their routine check.

I remember lots more noise. Beeping. Raised voices. Then—

"Chloe, are you awake? Eve's ready for a visit." A nurse held Chloe's arm around a small bundle wrapped in the standard pink-and-blue-striped receiving blanket. "There you go."

Another nurse snapped several photographs as mother and child seemed to stare at each other. "Eli and Trixie, squeeze in there close so this little miracle will see how special her family thinks she is when she gets older."

Family? A yearning so strong she couldn't speak silenced Beatrix's intended denial and her hesitation at stepping closer.

Chloe smiled, suddenly more alert than only a minute ago. "I'm gone to be wi' your daddy shoon an' tell him we made a perfick dauder. Eli'll take good care of you. Ish okay to call Trick-shee Mommy."

"Mommy?" Beatrix nearly choked on the word. As much as she longed for a child of her own, her practical side knew better than to believe the barely coherent statement of a woman in Chloe's condition. Accepting it as truth would only lead to another devastating loss.

I have to get out of here.

"Hold her, Trick-shee."

With Eli blocking her escape, Beatrix fought to calm the pulse hammering in her ears. Holding her nieces and nephews right after their births always agitated her old wound, but holding Eve with a promise of motherhood—real or not—would rip it wide open. "I—"

"Got her?" The nurse placed Eve's tiny body into the crook of Beatrix's free arm.

Instinct refused to listen to common sense, and she touched her nose to the full head of dark hair, letting the fine silk tickle her cheek. The intoxicating scent of baby filled her senses. What she wouldn't give to mother this child who would become an orphan within days.

A soft cry broke the spell, but it set off an intense urge to comfort Eve.

Eli caressed the baby's cheek and she quieted. "I need to go make some phone calls."

Thankful for the chance to escape before she got too attached, Beatrix turned to locate the nurse.

Chloe reached toward her. "Shtay, Trick-shee?"

A tangled mess of emotions drowned her even as Beatrix rejoiced at the chance to spend a little more time with the baby.

Eli gave her hand a gentle squeeze before releasing it. "Will you stay with Chloe? I won't be gone long."

Against her better judgment, Beatrix nodded. "Okay, I'll stay."

"Thank you." The gratitude in his eyes almost made her wish he'd stroke his fingers along her cheek with the same gentleness he'd shown Eve. He pulled his cell phone from his pocket as he headed for the exit. "I'll be back as quick as I can."

This is crazy. I probably won't ever see any of them again after today. Why am I here?

Eve let out another tiny yell and struggled to put her fist in her mouth. After two near misses, she gave a longer, louder cry. Beatrix swayed and bounced the way she often did to soothe her brothers' and sisters' kids, but the breathless cries continued.

"She wans to nursh." Chloe's observation brought her cousin's awkward question from last night to mind.

"Maybe I should ask the nurse for a bot—"

"No. You."

Beatrix tensed at a sudden tingling in her breasts, much like the feeling her sisters had described when feeding time approached. How many times had the ghost effect reminded her of the greatest loss she'd suffered?

Fighting panic, she offered the only excuse she could. "Look, I can't breastfeed her. I can't even have a baby."

Chloe pursed her lips. "Eve belongsh wi' you an' Eli. You can. You haf to wan to."

Desperate not to fall for the fantasy Chloe painted, Beatrix turned to the nurse who had placed Eve in her arms. "Can you get a bottle for her?"

The woman smiled. "Mama's right, you know. It's possible to induce lactation, even in women who can't have children. Ideally, you would've started the process several weeks ago, but we can make it work with some supplementing until you start producing your own milk. Have a seat and I'll help you get comfortable."

"But…" What if she could? What if the pang in her heart wasn't the wound that hadn't healed? What if it was yearning?

Sitting came too easily, as did adjusting her clothing to give the baby access to her left breast. The moment Eve latched on, Beatrix lost the will to pretend she could refuse Chloe's wishes or walk away from this miraculous child.

How Eli would fit into the picture she had no idea, nor did it matter. She might have misjudged him, but his interest in her had likely been motivated only by his need for a parenting partner—at least in the long term. Their almost sexual encounter this morning didn't mean anything, either. People had sex all the time without loving, or even liking, each other. Besides, they'd butted heads before the sparks had turned hot during the service call.

She could live without Eli as a husband, but she needed him to let her care for the child he'd agreed to raise.

"You're a natural, honey. Just think about bonding with her and nourishing her little body. Breastfeeding needs an emotional trigger more than a physical one to work." The nurse offered her a cup of water. "You should get in the habit of having something to drink while she's nursing. You'll need to stay hydrated."

Beatrix reached for the cup without looking up from the gray-blue gaze that seemed locked on her face. *Oh, Eve, I want to take you home.*

"I'll make sure the lactation consultant has a supplemental nursing system ready for you to use next time. She can also help you with placement of the feeding tube, figuring out a nursing schedule, and any questions you might have. She'll probably send a pump home with you too."

Next time. Please don't be a dream. "Okay."

"Let's switch sides in about two minutes. We don't want you to get sore on the first try." The nurse stepped away from the chair. "Still doing okay, Chloe?"

A long stretch of silence brought Beatrix's gaze to the bed. *Don't let her die yet!*

Chloe's eyes opened and a half smile suggested she was in no pain. She seemed to focus on her daughter. "Thank you, Trick-shee."

Beatrix didn't try to stop uncontrollable tears rolling down her cheeks. "Thank *you*, Chloe. I promise to take good care of her and tell her about her brave and wonderful mommy."

"An' Eli? He neesh you too."

A snort tried to escape. The man could probably use a keeper, but they were practically strangers. "You know we met yesterday, right? The only reason I'm here is because I was at his house for a plumbing job when you called. We don't even know each other well enough to be friends."

"You shtayed."

"I don't know why I stayed. It doesn't make sense."

"Con-neck-shun. Fate."

Timing. That's all. I would've done the same for anyone. "I'll help him the best I can with Eve. Um, I should probably switch sides now."

She shifted her clothes and the baby, hoping the distraction proved effective. The last thing she needed in her life was a complicated relationship, and Elijah Clayton confused the hell out of her. He might be part of a package deal, but that didn't mean she had to play house with him, at least not in the conventional way.

The door behind her opened and the devil walked in, his jaw more tense than last night after she'd called him a pervert. He stopped at the bed. "Both our parents will be here on the first available flight out of Denver. Brian's mother is driving down now. I had to tell them about the tumor. Is there anything else I need to do?"

"Lor-er."

He leaned closer to Chloe. "I don't understand."

"Trick-shee. Lah-er."

"Lawyer? You want to talk to the lawyer about Trixie? Okay. I'll call him right away."

Lawyer? Beatrix grabbed for Eli's shirt as he pulled his cell phone from his pocket again. "Wait a minute. What's this about a lawyer?"

"The guardianship. The lawy—" He pivoted toward her and immediately spun back around. "You… I didn't realize… Um, the, uh, lawyer set up a…um, guardianship for Eve. We talked about…adding a name to it if I…met someone."

"What are you stuttering about? It's not like you've never seen my breasts before." Suddenly aware that at least two of the nurses were watching—and undoubtedly listening to—the exchange, she lowered her voice. "And what, exactly, does *met someone* mean?"

His noisy exhale hinted that he wasn't any more comfortable defining what he meant than seeing her naked breasts. "Chloe wants you to be Eve's legal mother. We'll share parenting responsibilities and decision-making. And we'll live together in Chloe and Brian's house, where I'm living now."

She ignored the pinch to her ego from his obvious lack of interest in her as a possible wife. So what if it was all Chloe's doing? Evidently, meeting a suitable mother had been his intent, not finding a person he wanted to marry. She'd gladly give up her nonexistent personal life for eighteen years of motherhood. "Tell the lawyer I want to read the paperwork before we make this legal."

He gave a curt nod as he backed his way past her. "Will you go with Eve to the nursery if I'm not back before the doctor finishes?"

"Of course." Did he honestly believe she'd ever let the baby out of her sight? "Shouldn't we all have matching wristbands or something?"

"I knew I was forgetting something. I'll ask if we can do that now." He waved over a nurse, and, within two minutes, all four of them had coordinating hospital bracelets. Before Beatrix could thank him, he headed out the door again. "I'll be back as soon as I set up a meeting with the lawyer."

At least he seems like a dependable guy. Much more reliable than Derek.

Yep. No comparison. That chapter is over and done.

She touched her thumb to Eve's outstretched hand and savored the robust grip of delicate fingers holding on like her life depended on it. Chloe was right. Fate had played a part in her introduction and subsequent meeting with Eli, but this child was the catalyst—not romance, love, or even sexual attraction. The interaction with him had been a means to an end. Only Eve mattered—and Chloe passing from the world knowing someone would cherish her baby.

Unless the guardianship papers contained weird conditions for custody, agreeing to the terms was a no-brainer.

"I'll do my best, Eve." Beatrix leaned forward and pressed her lips to the smooth, warm skin on her precious gift's forehead. "How about another visit with your mommy?"

Having spent the last decade surrounded by nursing nieces and nephews, she made quick work of easing Eve free and covering herself.

As she stood, the doctor stepped from behind the draped sheet. "You're all set to head to your room, Chloe. Great job. I've ordered pain medication for you, but you let the nurses know if we need to raise the dosage like we talked about. You shouldn't have any pain."

Beatrix moved closer to the bed, hoping to delay the coming separation of mother and child. "Can she hold Eve again first?"

The doctor's smile seemed far more reconciled than happy. "That's a great idea."

Although Chloe's eyes were closed, her lips curved slightly upward when Beatrix laid her daughter in the crook of her arm the way the nurse had done. They both sighed, as if they suspected this was likely the final time they would be nestled together as one.

Warm breath tickled Beatrix's ear. *Eli.*

"The lawyer will be here in about half an hour." His hand wrapped around hers, bringing unexpected comfort to her breaking heart. "I wouldn't have been able to do this by myself."

The urge to bury her face in his shoulder and cry almost won, but she bit the inside of her cheek and focused on the pain. He was much stronger than he gave himself credit for.

He's stronger than I am. "I guess we'll never know, will we?"

Before she could suggest he take a turn holding Eve, the nurse positioned a bassinet next to them. "Let's take this little girl to the nursery for her bath and a few routine tests while her mama gets settled back in her room."

Beatrix reluctantly lifted the baby from Chloe's loose hold and handed her to the nurse. Then she kissed Eli on the cheek before she overthought the simple gesture. "I'm glad I was here for you."

A hint of color crept up his neck. "Um, I'll come find you when the, uh, lawyer gets here."

After a quick nod, she hurried from the room behind the nurse and her precious cargo. The walk was just long enough to let her mind wander to Eli's reaction to her innocent peck on his day-old beard. The poor man had acted like he'd never been kissed—not at all like their hot-and-heavy almost-sex encounter. He was an enigma.

Sweet yet prickly. Cute but standoffish. Sometimes awkward and other times more normal than me. Can I survive living in the same house with him?

She stopped at the viewing window when the nurse entered the nursery. Instead of the usual wistful ache that came with seeing everyone else's newborns, sadness and wonder mixed with guilty excitement. This time, she would take home a baby, but Chloe wouldn't go home at all.

Her phone buzzed against her hip, pulling her from what could easily have become an emotional tug of war. Even Shelley's nosy questions were preferable to a battle with no winner.

She checked the screen and barely refrained from groaning.

"What are doing at the hospital? Are you hurt?"

"I had to drive a guy I know—" She tapped the delete button and chose her words more carefully. "*So now you're spying on me? A friend had a family emergency and needed a ride. Tell Maddie I'm not going to make it over to replumb the bathroom today. Maybe this weekend? A really big job has come up."*

Her sister would find out soon enough what the job entailed, and "big" didn't begin to cover it. The pressure to date might even disappear.

"Woo-hoo! Maddie won't be happy, but yay for you anyway! Hope everything's okay with your friend."

"I'll tell you all about it soon. Gotta go." She pocketed her phone and located the new light of her life on the other side of the glass.

Telling her family about Eve didn't worry her, but her relationship with Eli would undoubtedly spark questions, most of which she had no idea how to answer.

CHAPTER FIVE

Eli paced eight long steps down the hallway and another eight the other direction, trying to understand why Beatrix affected him the way she did. If he closed his eyes, he could imagine the softness of her kiss on his cheek. His palms still tingled where they'd touched her breasts this morning.

I almost had sex with her.

God, how he'd wanted that physical connection to her, to forget everything for a while. No amount of analyzing could make sense of that reaction.

He shoved his fists in his pockets and pivoted to the right, coming face to face with the lawyer. "Mr. Lathrop."

"Eli." The older man seemed to have aged several years since their last meeting only a few weeks ago. "How's Chloe?"

The vise on Eli's chest tightened. "She's a lot worse today. She started slurring and her blood-oxygen levels are down. She talked about seeing Brian soon."

With a hand on Eli's shoulder, the lawyer sighed. "I'm so sorry. And the baby? Is she healthy?"

"Eve is fine. She looks like Chloe." The lump in Eli's throat tightened. "Should we go to the nursery for Beatrix?"

Mr. Lathrop turned toward the entrance to the room. "If Chloe's up to it, I'd like to talk to her first. I want her to confirm what you told me on the phone, just to cover all the bases."

"I'll ask if we can go in yet." Eli took a fortifying breath and knocked on the door.

One of day-shift orderlies opened it several inches. "G'morning, Mr. Clayton. I was just about to see if you wanted to come in while Chloe's awake."

"Yes. Is it okay if Mr. Lathrop comes in with me?"

The man stepped aside as he widened the opening. "Doc said to let you make the call on visitors, that you won't let anybody rile her up."

"Okay." Eli nodded at the lawyer and led him to his cousin's bedside. The tension eased from his shoulders when she looked up at him, but the ashen tone of her face brought it back again. "Mr. Lathrop is here about adding Beatrix to the guardianship papers. Are you sure that's what you want to do?"

Her mouth moved, but no sound came out.

Breathe. Focus. "You don't have to talk. Can you blink once for yes or twice for no?"

She closed and reopened her eyelids in slow motion. Wanting to be certain of her answer, he waited the count of twenty for more movement.

Mr. Lathrop patted her hand. "That's confirmation enough for me. You can rest easy, Chloe. Since we already had the paperwork drawn up for this contingency, it's just a matter of Eli and Miss Glouster signing the codicil." He withdrew an envelope from the inside pocket of his suit coat and offered it to Eli. "I brought a copy for you both to look over. And I'll sign as a witness, of course. I've asked one of the paralegals from the office to serve as a second witness. She's on her way up. Would you like me to sit with Chloe while you get your fiancée?"

Unsure how to respond to the lawyer's assumption, Eli took the paperwork and stepped toward the exit. "Um, yes, I'll get Beatrix."

He hurried along the hallway toward the elevators, intent on finalizing the last of his cousin's wishes before she slipped into the inevitable coma she wouldn't wake from. If Chloe had no misgivings, he had no right to doubt her. He wouldn't be left on his own to care for her daughter and, for that, he'd forfeit a good part of his comfort zone.

The doors slid open as he reached to push the call button. A nurse backed out of the elevator, guiding a wheeled contraption like the one Eve had been placed in to go to the nursery.

Beatrix exited behind the nurse, her hand inside the rolling baby bed. Her head popped up a second before she bumped into him. As she scooted sideways around him, her breast grazed his bicep. "Oh, Elijah! Sorry, I wasn't watching where I was going. Is the lawyer here?"

He rubbed his palm along his upper arm, hoping to banish the feel of her nipple against his skin before he developed an erection like the one she'd inspired earlier. "Uh, the lawyer. Yes, he's here."

"Do you have the guardianship papers?" She gestured for him to follow her. "I asked about letting Eve stay with Chloe until…you know. So they can spend more time together. Are those the papers in your hand?"

"Darn it." He fell into step beside her. "We talked to the doctors about that a couple weeks ago. I forgot to ask today."

"Don't beat yourself up. It's been a stressful day." Her sympathetic reassurance caught him off guard, reminding him of their initial meeting and his certainty that he'd found the right woman to become his partner. "The papers?"

"Hm? Yeah." He pointed to a sitting area as they neared the room. "Would you mind if we read them over there? Then we can talk without disturbing Chloe and Eve. When we're done, I'll tell Mr. Lathrop we're ready to sign them."

She frowned at him. "You haven't read them yet?"

"Chloe told me what they say, but I didn't need to read them until now." Perching on the edge of the couch, he leaned forward to rest his chin on his fist. "I've been prepping for classes, teaching, going to faculty meetings, and trying to put in research time. I couldn't be there for all the legal stuff, too. Do you know what it's like to watch somebody who's dying change a will, put guardianship provisions in place, and plan a funeral?"

"Okay, point taken. I'm just nervous about this…arrangement. I wasn't exactly expecting a stranger to ask me to raise her child today." Her noisy sigh summed up his exhaustion and frustration perfectly. "Come on. Let's see what it says."

Too stressed to unfold the papers, let alone read them, he handed the envelope to her. "Here."

She ran her fingertips along the top crease several times. "Ready?"

"Do I have a choice?"

"Not really." The papers crinkled as she pulled them from the envelope and unfolded them. Then she sat beside him, close enough that her arm touched his.

He straightened, hoping to put a little space between them. The cushion shifted beneath him and he narrowly missed grabbing her thigh to keep from falling on her. "Uh, sorry. Maybe I should sit in the chair."

She grasped his chin, forcing him to look her in the eye. "I won't bite. Besides, we can't both read if you're sitting over there. Now relax and let's get this done."

Annoyed with her ability to gauge his mood, he leaned back and put his arm around her. "You're bossy."

"When I need to be." She nestled closer and rested her head on his collarbone. "Shut up and read."

Her tone had softened, but he had no idea how to decipher what she meant. He turned his attention to the legal document she held instead of prolonging his discomfort.

Halfway through the first page of heretofores and hereupons, a single sentence stopped his progress. *"The original designated guardian, Elijah M. Clayton, Jr., and his chosen co-guardian, Beatrix Glouster, shall marry no later than fourteen days after the birth of Evelyn Brianna Long, daughter of Chloe Evelyn Long and the late Brian James Long, in order to maintain shared guardianship."*

Although marriage had been his plan during the weeks of meeting potential candidates, he hadn't thought about his cousin choosing someone for him because the woman happened to be present at the last possible moment.

Beatrix gasped, probably from the same sentence. "I was looking for a serious relationship, but this says we have two weeks to take the plunge! So in order to become Eve's mother, I have to marry you by the eighteenth?"

Appalled by her horrified tone, he untangled himself from her and pushed to his feet. "You don't have to make it sound so—so distasteful. And nobody's forcing you."

"Oh, really? You think I can walk away from her after what just happened?" She slapped the papers onto the couch. "I don't believe this. You had to have known about—"

"What do you mean I can't go in? I want to see my granddaughter. And my daughter-in-law."

Mrs. Long? How did she get here so fast?

"Where's Elijah?" His stomach cramped at Chloe's mother-in-law's tone. "I need to find out when I can pick up the baby's things from my son's house. I'll need the crib and clothes and everything when I take her home."

Papers crinkled and Beatrix growled behind him. Her fingers closed around his wrist and she pulled him toward the hall, even as she whispered beside him. "Nobody's taking Eve anywhere. Come on. We're signing. Right now."

"Elijah, there you are!" Mrs. Long greeted him with an almost-kiss on the cheek. "Why won't they let me in to see Chloe and the baby? I'm *so* distraught over her illness, but thank goodness the baby is okay."

"I, uh…"

Beatrix stepped between him and Brian's mother. "She has a visitor right now. Eli, why don't we go see if he's almost done with his visit?" Before he could answer, she eased open the door, giving him no option but to follow her. She stopped at the tray table that had been pushed against the wall. "Mr. Lathrop, do you have a pen I can borrow?"

The lawyer and a woman Eli recognized from Mr. Lathrop's office rose from the chairs beside the bed. "You're ready to sign?"

"Yes. In blood, if necessary." Even as terrible as he was at interpreting inflections and body language, the decisiveness in her answer left no doubt in Eli's mind that Beatrix meant what she said.

"No need for that." Lathrop removed a pen from his pocket and handed it to her. "I heard raised voices in the hallway. Is everything okay?"

"It will be, once this is done." Beatrix moved the tip across the paper, leaving her signature flowing along the co-guardian line on all the copies. She set the pen on the tray and hurried toward the bassinet. "Your turn, Elijah."

Her sudden conviction didn't settle his nerves, but it did support Chloe's confidence that Beatrix would be a good mother. Having to trust his own instincts was always much less reassuring.

He picked up the pen with a shaky hand and scrawled his barely legible name next to hers. Hopefully, a mandatory wedding was the only surprise.

Mr. Lathrop wasted no time signing on the line below their signatures and passed the copies to his paralegal. "This is what she wants—a loyal young woman for you and the baby. Keep a copy with you for when Eve is released from the hospital. I'll also email you a copy and put another in the mail as soon as I get back to the office."

"Thank you. I'll call you when…" Unable to complete the awful thought, Eli dropped his chin to his chest.

"You can call me any time for anything. Knowing what's going to happen doesn't make it less difficult." The older man patted Eli's back. "Walk me to the elevator?"

"Sure." As Eli opened the door, Mrs. Long blocked the exit.

"Can I go in now?" She leaned to the side, peeking around him into the room. "Do you know how soon the hospital will release the baby to me? Oh, and when's a good time to get the keys to the house? I need to set up an appointment with a real estate agent."

The lawyer extended his hand and offered her a business card, drawing her gaze from Eli and the paralegal. "I'm John Lathrop. I represent Chloe's legal interests. I'll need to see documentation of your claims before you can take custody of the baby or ownership of the house."

Her frown seemed more irritated than sad. "Documentation? I'm the baby's grandmother. I believe that makes me the next of kin. I'm exercising my right to raise her and use my judgment on how to best provide for her."

"I have legal documents that state otherwise. If you have your lawyer call me, I'll be glad to answer any questions. Would you excuse me a moment while I speak to Mr. Clayton?" He stepped back into the room, nudging Eli with him. The door swung silently closed. "How do you feel about moving up the wedding date? My gut says Mrs. Long will try to use anything and everything to get her hands on Eve and the estate, including the fact that you and Miss Glouster aren't married yet."

"She can't take Eve, can she?" Eli shoved his hands through his hair, hoping Beatrix couldn't hear the conversation. Her rush to sign the papers and check on the baby had to mean something important.

Mr. Lathrop shook his head. "No. I'll make sure the hospital staff knows who her legal guardians are."

"Okay." *What else should I ask?* "How soon do we need to get married?"

"Ideally, before Chloe passes away and Eve is released from the hospital. Sometime today or tomorrow morning is my best advice."

A surge of anxiety pulsed through Eli's veins, but a deep breath relieved some of the worry coursing through his body. "I don't know how to get married. Don't we need a permit or something? And she might want a fancy dress. How do I find a minister or a judge?"

"I'll contact a friend about officiating if you and Beatrix go to the probate office for the license right away. You'll need your driver's license and your social security number." Mr. Lathrop glanced toward the other side of the room. "Why don't you talk to her about this before I leave? We wouldn't want her to think she doesn't have any say in the matter."

With a nod, Eli walked to the woman who would likely be his wife by tomorrow afternoon. *What if she changes her mind? What if she doesn't?*

She adjusted Eve's blanket as he approached. "She's beautiful, isn't she? We can go after her feeding. The lactation consultant should be here any minute."

"Go where?" Whatever plans she had would have to wait until they handled the immediate issue of their marital status.

Beatrix raised her eyebrows at him, like he should know what she was talking about. "To get the license? We can grab some lunch when we're done at the courthouse. I'll pay for parking and lunch if you'll take care of the license fee."

"How can you be so calm about all of this? And how did you know what I was going to ask?" A new knot formed at the base of his neck.

"Having a meltdown won't help. I made the decision to sign the papers, knowing the conditions. What difference does it make if we get married this afternoon or two weeks from now?" She lifted Eve from her portable bed. "I have very good hearing. Sit. You haven't held her yet."

"I've never held a baby." Crossing his arms in front of his chest, he backed away. "What if I drop her or she cries?"

"Elijah Clayton, I'm not spending the next eighteen years with someone who thinks I should do all the parenting. You promised to be a father to Eve. That means comforting her when she's fussy and helping her go back to sleep when wakes up in the middle of the night." She motioned toward the chair with her head. "You can do this. Now sit."

"Okay." With his heart hammering and his hands shaking, he sat.

"Relax. And breathe. Bend your elbow so you have a place to support her head." She positioned Eve in the crook of his arm and guided his other hand around her to form a cradle. "Just like that."

Sleepy eyes blinked open and a dainty yawn followed. Warmth seeped through his shirt where she lay against him. "She's so light."

Eve's tiny mouth curved upward as she seemed to study his face.

Beatrix giggled, sending his insides cartwheeling. "She likes you."

"Or she's laughing at me because I don't know what I'm doing."

"Nope. She likes you." His future wife's eyes locked on his. "You've been taking care of her and Chloe, and she knows you're a good person. I bet she even recognizes your voice."

His pulse did the same thump-thump-thump it had the first time he'd met this woman. "She could hear me before she was born?"

"Yeah." Beatrix's gaze shifted away from his. "There's the lactation consultant. If you'd rather not stay while I feed Eve, you could go find my clothes since I didn't have a chance to change out of the scrubs yet."

Grateful for the excuse to escape seeing Beatrix's breasts again, he stood. "That'll save us some time when you're done. It's not that I don't like… Forget I said that."

"Not a chance." Beatrix grinned at him as she scooped the baby from his arms. "Remind me that we need to stop at my condo on the way to the courthouse. I need to pick up something."

Hoping the heat creeping up his neck faded quickly, he tried to ignore his embarrassing admission. "Mr. Lathrop said we only have to have a driver's license and social security number to apply. What do you need to pick up?"

Her gaze met his again for a second and then darted away. The smile became a grimace. "My divorce decree."

CHAPTER SIX

THE NEUTRAL EXPRESSION ON ELI'S FACE OFFERED NO CLUE ABOUT HIS thoughts, leaving Beatrix to assume he was less than thrilled to discover she had a previous marriage. He was hardly the first man to pass judgment on her since she and Derek had split.

She hid the twinge of hurt and anger behind a smile as she greeted the lactation consultant. "Hi. You must be Lois. The maternity nurses said you'd help me with the supplemental nursing system and have a pump for me to take home. Eli, why don't you go get my clothes?"

With a curt nod, he hurried out of the room like her past was something he could escape.

Go ahead. Run away. See if I care.

Settling in the chair he'd vacated, she blocked his reaction from her mind and concentrated on the task at hand. "Okay. Let's do this."

Half an hour and only a single mishap later, she pulled her scrub top down and lifted Eve's head to her shoulder. "That wasn't so bad. I can probably get the hang of it."

Lois gathered the plastic bag and tubing. "You did great. Just remember the cleaning instructions we talked about. Do you have any questions about the breast pump?"

"I don't think—"

"—here for forty-five minutes." Mrs. Long pushed past Eli as he entered the room. "I refuse to wait any longer. Where is she? I want to see my granddaughter."

With his attention focused toward the floor, he followed her. "We aren't interrupting, um, anything, are we?"

Beatrix pressed her lips to the tuft of dark hair tickling her chin. "We just finished, didn't we, Eve? Clean diaper and a full tummy."

With a scowl that aged her face at least ten years, Mrs. Long rounded the bed, not even glancing toward her dying daughter-in-law. "Why wasn't I allowed to come in and feed her? I have half a mind to —" She froze mid-step at the bassinet. "A breast pump? Chloe can't possibly be in any condition to…"

A frown marked the moment she seemed to comprehend the situation. She finally looked toward the bed and then buried her face in her hands. Her shoulders trembled as she sobbed.

Eli clutched a bag to his chest, looking ready to bolt out the door again if he could make his feet move.

I'm on my own, am I?

Dead son. Dying daughter-in-law. Someone else raising her granddaughter. Yep, I can work up some sympathy.

Beatrix guided the older woman to the chair. "Would you like to hold Eve? We didn't mean to keep you from seeing her. It's just been a really stressful day so far and it doesn't promise to get any better."

"It—it's like the day Brian d-died, without a baby." Mrs. Long plucked a tissue from her purse and dabbed at the spots marring her flawless makeup. Her gaze shifted toward the bed and then toward Eve. "I should've come down to visit more often, but it's so hard to go out of the house some days. That poor girl. She lost her husband, and now…"

"You know what? Would you mind sitting with Eve and Chloe while Eli and I grab some lunch and run a quick errand? I'm Beatrix, by the way, but you can call me Trixie if you want."

The hopeful look in her eyes convinced Beatrix that they might actually come to agreeable visitation terms without legal action. "I'm Nancy. May I?"

Beatrix placed the baby in Mrs. Long's outstretched arms.

"Oh, she has Brian's ears and forehead." Nancy sniffled and traced the delicate curve of Eve's ear. "That hair is all Chloe, though. Did she get to hold her?"

"Yes, twice in the operating room. We don't know if she'll wake up enough to hold her again or not, but they're together. That's all that matters right now."

"She would've been a wonderful mother. Life's so unfair sometimes."

"It can be. I should get changed so Eli and I can go." Rather than dwelling on the enduring ache in her heart, Beatrix hurried to the restroom, grabbing the bag of clothes from her silent soon-to-be husband on the way.

She peeled off her top and then untied the drawstring at her waist. As the pants fell to her ankles, she ran her fingertip along the faded scar at her bikini line. *I guess I don't ever have to worry about explaining this.*

Between her marital and medical history, she wouldn't have expected him to freak out over the less drastic of the two. Of course, he probably didn't plan on seeing that part of her now that she had the dreaded D attached to her name—if he had to begin with.

She dragged her T-shirt over her head and checked the mirror to be sure it was on right side out and frontward.

A plumber and an English professor walk into a marriage for the wrong reasons. And baby makes three. There's a bad joke if I ever heard one.

A deep breath didn't calm the butterflies in her stomach.

And I'm gonna do it anyway.

Leaving the scrubs on the sink, she exited the bathroom with as much confidence as she could muster. "Nancy, I really appreciate you staying here. We'll be back in time for Eve's next feeding. Can we bring you anything? Lunch? Coffee?"

The older woman looked up from her armful and smiled. "Yes, coffee would be nice. Thank you."

"One coffee. See you soon." Beatrix tugged on Eli's sleeve. "Ready to go?"

Without a word, he led the way out of the room and down the hall, his spine straight and stiff the entire way. The elevator opened as he reached for the button, shortening the awkward moments of silence by a few seconds. Even as she walked beside him out of the hospital and to the parking garage, he didn't speak.

Okay. This is annoying.

As much as she hated confrontations and could probably safely assume he did too from his behavior, the divorce issue wasn't something they could ignore if they were going to share a house.

When we get to the condo, we're having a chat, mister, whether you like it or not.

She slid behind the wheel of her truck and started the engine. The click of their seat belts sounded in unison, but it seemed more like a wall going up between them than their lives being in sync.

Shadows flickered through the cab as she circled down to street level. At the self-service machine, she inserted the parking stub, swiped her credit card, and counted the seconds until the crossing arm rose. It finally wobbled upward. After the constant noise in the hospital, the deathly quiet ate at her last nerve on the eight-minute drive home.

She parked at the end of the sidewalk leading to her front door. "Come inside."

His jaw flexed, but he followed her into the condo and upstairs to her bedroom.

Instead of pulling the security box out of the closet and shuffling through the papers, she rested her hip against the edge of the dresser. "I don't like games, Eli. Out with it."

"Um, okay." He dragged down his zipper and unbuttoned his trousers. Then he pushed his pants and boxers past his narrow hips. His half-erect dick swung upward to point directly at her.

"What are you doing?" A spasm in her lower belly chased away her conviction to lecture him on the reasons people divorced. "Oh. Out with it. I didn't mean it literally. But that works too. Condoms are in the nightstand. The one next to you."

Anticipation set her heart racing as he pulled on the drawer handle. Sex might prove an effective distraction from life, death, and a quickie wedding, not to mention the heartache and disappointments in her past. She deserved an escape, didn't she?

Something rattled when he reached inside. He jerked his hand back and looked over his shoulder toward her. His pink cheeks hinted at what he'd found.

"Aw, come on. It's just a vibrator and a supply of batteries. Get the condom or put that erection away." *Wait a minute. I'm going to be married to this guy. A little test run isn't too much to ask.* She peeled off her shirt and tossed it on the floor. With her fingers poised to unhook her bra, she gave him her best come-hither look. "Actually, don't you dare put that thing away. Get the condom and we'll figure out which parts of me you're willing to admit you like."

The blush spread to his neck and ears, but he retrieved a blue packet instead of pulling up his pants.

She flicked open the front closure, careful not to allow the cups to slip free. "If you're sure you want to do this, finish undressing and put on the rubber."

He wasted no time kicking off his shoes and shedding the rest of his clothes. His pectoral muscles flexed as he tore the edge from the package, triggering a pulse through her clit. With methodical slowness, he rolled the latex sheath into place. His jutting hard-on bobbed up and down when he reached the base.

"Sit on the bed with your back against the pillows and tell me which parts you like as I take off my clothes." A slight shift in her posture sent the straps sliding down her arms. She arched and let the cups fall. The cool air chilled her nipples.

"Those." The word came out on a squeak.

"What are they called?" She'd get him to loosen up and learn to communicate with her if they had to go through this routine every day for the next ten years. "You get bonus points for creativity."

He squirmed against the pillows. "Breasts. Um, boobs? I don't like that word. It makes them sound stupid. I…like your nipples. They remind me of raspberries."

"Very good." She removed her boots. "Do you want to touch them again?"

The comforter bunched and wrinkled around his fists. "Yes."

She shimmied out of her jeans and panties, taking full advantage of the opportunity to bend over. The half choke, half groan behind her brought a swell of satisfaction. "Tell me, Eli. Use your words."

"You have a pretty…bottom."

"You can do better than that." She bent forward again, this time spreading her legs to give him a peek at more than her backside.

His whimper spoke of a man about to take matters into his own hands. "Can we just have sex now?"

Taking pity on him, she crawled onto the bed and straddled his thighs. "Don't you want to touch me first?"

He leaned forward until their mouths met, and he snaked his tongue past her lips. Each forceful glide pushed her closer to forgoing the foreplay she always needed and giving him exactly what he wanted. He cupped her breasts, his thumbs and forefingers closing around her already taut nipples.

Sparks of electricity zinged southward from the point of origin, igniting a fire that threatened to burn her from the inside out. She whimpered as she guided his cock into place.

He rolled her onto the covers and drove into her in a single quick thrust, stretching and filling her far better than a vibrator. His moan echoed hers as she broke the kiss long enough for a breath. Then she battled with his tongue again, wresting control from him until he moved again.

The second thrust stole her breath, and she hooked her legs around his waist to prolong the wonderful agony of near release. He pumped into her again and again, setting off round after round of preliminary fireworks. Each time carried her closer to what promised to be a truly amazing orgasm. As he tensed above her and groaned, the dam finally let loose and a surge of blissful pleasure washed over her.

With her heart thumping in her chest and bells ringing in her ears, she dragged him down on top of her. His weight comforted rather than stifled, reminding her how lonely sleeping alone could be. She smoothed her hands over the hard planes of his shoulder blades and savored the rhythmic sound of their breathing.

"Is it always like this?" The practicality and wonder in Eli's voice sent her stomach cartwheeling.

Oh my God. Was he a virgin?

The thought made answering his question impossible, so she shook her head. Sex had never been that urgent or mutually satisfying with her ex or either of the other two men she'd slept with after the divorce.

Why did he choose me?

His breath tickled her ear. "Is that good? Did you like it?"

He honestly couldn't tell?

She tightened her arms around him and kissed his collarbone. "Very good."

"Would you want to do it again? Not right away. Later. I mean, since we're going to be married, we could do what married people do. I found two boxes of condoms in Chloe and Brian's bedroom when I moved my stuff in there."

His awkward explanation was giggle-worthy, but she wasn't about to risk offending him or making him clam up. Besides, if he wanted a real marriage, she could live with that. He did, however, deserve the truth prior to the exchanging of vows. "I'd like that, but there's something you should know before we spend money on a license."

He pushed up on his elbows and frowned. "You can't back out now. What did I do wrong? I'll fix it. I promise."

She sighed. "It's me. And you can't fix it."

"I don't care, whatever it is." His frown became a calculated smirk. "Eve needs you."

Impressed with his ability to play the guilt card, she almost laughed. "Roll off. I want to show you something."

He did as she asked, lying on his side facing her. "I like all the parts I see and I'll call them whatever you want me to."

"Eli, listen to me. Please? This is important." She used his finger to trace the scar along her lower belly. "See that? Once upon a time, I was married. And my husband and I decided to have a baby. I got pregnant right away and everything seemed to be going fine. Then, when I was a little more than five months along, the placenta pulled away from the uterine wall. I had to have an emergency C-section. My baby died. My husband left me."

"The divorce decree." The green faded from his hazel eyes, leaving only brown. "At the hospital, when I tried to make you feel Eve kick. And you went in the operating room with me. How could he *leave* you after something like that?"

She shrugged, less concerned with why Derek had abandoned her than how Eli might react to the rest of her revelation. "During the surgery, there were complications. I had to have a partial hysterectomy. I can't have children. Eve is it for us, unless we adopt or use a surrogate."

He rolled to his back and laid his forearm across his face. Then he laughed, a sound so hurtful she wanted to curl into a ball and disappear.

The bed creaked as he sat up and scooted off the bed. He paced toward the doorway and then retraced his steps back to the nightstand.

Just leave already. Get it over with so I can move on with my life. Again.

He removed the condom and wrapped it in a tissue before dropping it in the wastebasket. "You can't get pregnant?"

Clinging to last of her dignity, she met his gaze. "No."

"And I don't have to wear a condom when we have sex?"

What is he talking about? "The only way we're having sex again is if we get married."

"Okay, but do I have to wear a condom?"

She rolled her eyes, too emotionally drained to maintain any control over her blunt nature. "If we were to have sex again, you wouldn't have to wear a condom, as long as you don't have any weird diseases. However, no marriage equals no more sex."

"You're the first. I've never. No diseases. We need to get dressed and drive to the courthouse." He picked up their clothes and sorted them into piles on the bed. "What do you want for lunch?"

Reaching for her underwear, she tried to make sense of the disjointed mishmash of his questions and statements. “You understand that we can’t make a baby together? At least not in the conventional way.”

With his shirt unbuttoned and his boxers at his knees, he scrunched up his face at her. “We already have a baby. Why would we need another one?”

CHAPTER SEVEN

ELI TUCKED HIS SHIRT INTO HIS PANTS, DOING HIS BEST NOT TO WATCH Beatrix dress. Every wiggle and stretch coaxed him to finagle another few minutes in bed with her. She'd shot his notion of having a platonic marriage to kingdom come.

His cell phone jangled as he bent to slip on his sock, throwing him off balance. He hopped on one foot toward the bed.

The hospital? Chloe? Not yet!

"Aren't you going to answer that?" The urgency in Beatrix's voice only added to his worry.

"I'm trying!" He lifted the phone to his ear, hoping for a telemarketing call. "Hello."

"Hello, Eli. This is John Lathrop. Judge Bradley is available at two thirty today. Can you and Miss Glouster meet me in the waiting area outside Chloe's room at twenty-five after?"

Relief calmed his rampant pulse. "We'll be there. Do we need anything besides the marriage license?"

"No. He's offered to officiate free of charge, considering the circumstances. I'd be honored to act as a witness, although witnesses aren't required."

"Okay." *What else should I ask?* Hoping he hadn't forgotten anything important, Eli gave up on his short-circuited thoughts. "Thank you for making the arrangements."

"Glad to help. See you soon."

Eli shoved his foot into his shoe and grabbed his second sock from the bed as he ended the call. Leaning against the edge of the mattress, he yanked on the sock and bent to tie his right shoe.

"Well?" The tip of Beatrix's boot tapped the floor in front of him.

"Well, what?" Glancing upward, he aimed for the other shoe.

She frowned at him. "You really need to learn how to communicate. I can guess who was on the phone by the context, but what did he say about the arrangements?"

After a tug on his sock to flatten a wrinkle, he tied his wingtip. "Mr. Lathrop arranged for someone to officiate. The judge will perform the ceremony at two thirty."

"*At two thirty?*" She plunked a metal box on the floor, narrowly missing his foot. "We have less than two hours to get the license, pick up lunch, and drive to… Where are we supposed to meet the judge?"

"The hospital."

"I guess that's better than traffic court." Shuffling through a stack of envelopes from the box, she set one after another aside. "It has to be here somewhere. Help me look."

He knelt next to her. "What am I looking for?"

"An envelope with a skull and crossbones drawn on it in black ink."

"You consider your ex-husband a pirate? The symbolism is fairly obvious."

She laughed and flipped through the last bunch of papers. "More like poison. He did his fair share of pillaging my feelings, but he was more of a spineless turd-face. Ah, I should've known. The bottom one. Right where he belongs. Ready to go?"

A spineless turd-face?

Her nonchalant attitude surprised him, but he stood and offered her a hand up instead of prolonging a discussion about her past. "Ready."

"Let's go then." She led him out of the bedroom, her bottom swaying as she walked.

How had he never noticed the way a woman's hips moved in that hypnotic motion?

Poetic.

Her fingertips skimmed the length of the banister as she hurried down the stairs, triggering a baser reaction than the simple need to describe her movements in lyrical meter. Emotion mixed with sexual attraction, a combination he'd never experienced before. Other than detached curiosity, he hadn't really been interested in sex until now.

She ushered him to the front door and pointed toward his zipper. "Do you think you can try not to have an erection at the courthouse and the hospital?"

Heat crept up his neck. "I can't help it. I keep picturing you without clothes. And how did you notice unless you were looking there?"

"It's kind of hard to miss." Her lips curved upward. "Besides, I didn't say *I* mind."

He weighed the urge to kiss her against the chance that now was the wrong time, the wrong place, or some other wrong factor. Jeopardizing his future with her over a biological response seemed foolish, especially when he should be focused on his cousin's wishes. "I'll do the best I can."

"I can't ask for more than that." She locked the door behind them and jangled the keys in her palm as they hurried along the sidewalk. "Do you mind if we pick up lunch on the way to the courthouse? I'm starving."

In an effort to make a good impression, he opened the driver's side door of her truck. "I'm hungry too. I didn't have a chance to eat breakfast this morning before the faucet exploded. And we still have to clean up that mess. The floor isn't going to collapse or something from the water, is it?"

"Shoot! I forgot all about the leak." As she climbed behind the steering wheel, a strange clucking sound came from inside the truck. "Mom, you have impeccable timing. Get in, Eli. I need you to answer that."

A bud of panic formed in his chest. "You want me to talk to your mom? After we…you know."

"You don't have to talk to my mom. I need you to type in an answer to her text message while I drive." She waved her hand at him like she was shooing a cat. "Just get in so we can pick up lunch and go to the courthouse. Two o'clock is going to get here too fast as it is."

"Okay." Glad she'd taken charge of the situation, he rounded the front end of the pickup. As he settled in the passenger seat, she laid her phone on his leg, her fingertips brushing his thigh and setting off a new batch of sensations in his testicles. He held his breath to keep from groaning.

"Sorry." Although she sounded sincere, her smile hinted that she was amused by his reaction. "How did a man like you stay a virgin for so long?"

"What do you mean, 'a man like me?'" He buckled his seat belt, hoping his face wasn't as red as it felt.

"No need to get to defensive. I just meant that you aren't exactly good at hiding your sexual responses to being touched by a woman." Turning toward the rear window, she backed out of the driveway. "Most men can't exercise that kind of control over their libidos."

The phone clucked again, making him jump and giving him the perfect opportunity to change the subject. "What am I supposed to say to your mom?"

"Read her message. She probably heard about me being at the hospital from my sister."

He caught a momentary glimpse of text before the screen went dark. "What's your password?"

"Eight-seven-four-nine-four-three."

"Trixie?" A quick tap of the numbers took him to a screen full of icons. "You should use something less obvious and more secure."

"How did you know what that meant?" She switched on her turn signal as she slowed for a red light.

"Know what *what* meant? 'How's your friend? Anything I can do to help?'"

"What? My friend? Oh, Mom's message. You remind me of my nephew. He can recite the value of pi to twenty decimal places, but sometimes he has no clue how to…" Her sideways glance at him lasted longer than was comfortable. "Eli, are you an Aspie?"

No.

Yes.

Do I tell her?

What if she changes her mind? Maybe I should—

"I mean, it's okay if you are, and it sure would explain some of the things you've said and done." When a car horn sounded, she finally looked away. "Oops. Light's green."

"I, um. What should I… How should I…" A cold sweat spread across his back and shoulders, and every semi-intelligent word vanished from his vocabulary. He gripped the edge of the seat to keep from wringing his hands. "Damn it."

"Deep breaths." Her palm closed over the back of his hand, soothing the panic racing through him. "It isn't important right now. Let's grab some lunch. Ian always seems to focus better on a full stomach. High metabolism and low blood sugar don't mix well with ASD. Add stress, and he's a basket case."

Relieved at not having to work so hard to hide what a lot of people considered a defect, he slowly inhaled. An equally slow exhale released most of the tightness in his body.

She breathed with him the second time. "I meant what I said. It's no big deal."

Grateful for her understanding, he flipped over his hand and linked his fingers with hers. The words still wouldn't flow from his thoughts to his mouth, but verbal confirmation hardly seemed necessary.

"Feeling better now?"

He shrugged, not sure she would feel the same weeks or months from now. That had been his biggest concern during his search for a wife. Spotting a restaurant he stopped at on occasion, he pointed with his free hand. "Let's get lunch there."

"Okay." She made the turn and pulled into a parking spot. The comforting weight of her touch vanished as she got out of the truck. "Why don't you wait here while I get food?"

The prospect of a few minutes with no pressure to admit the truth was too good to pass up, so he nodded. "A number five, hot. With no onions and just a little bit of mustard. No, they always put on too much. Get the mustard on the side. Never mind. No mustard."

"Number five. Hot. No onions. No mustard. Oh, and a please would be nice next time. Tell my mom that my friend is going through a rough patch right now, so I'm going to hang around for a while. Ask if she has time to do me a favor. I'll be back in a few minutes." She shoved the door closed and jogged toward the entrance to the building.

Her ponytail bounced up and down above her jeans-clad bottom, almost distracting him from his task. *Eight-seven-four-nine-four-three.*

The screen of icons appeared again and he opened the text message app.

"My friend is going through a rough patch right now, so I'm going to hang around for a while. Do you have time to do me a favor? I'll be back in a few minutes."

He tapped the Send button and waited for the message to pop up in the conversation. Then he called his cell so he could add her number to his contacts and his to hers. All his married colleagues seemed to know their spouses' phone numbers, and fitting in made him closer to normal. Even if the circumstances weren't quite traditional, he and Beatrix would be husband and wife in two hours.

As he typed her name into his phone, the one on his leg clucked. Why had she chosen the sound of a chicken?

The door swung open and Beatrix set a bag on the console as she climbed in. "I got a bottle of water and a bottle of apple juice since I didn't know what you usually drink. Did my mom answer yet?"

"I think so. Is she the only one who clucks?" He handed her the phone.

"Mm-hm. She's my mother hen." After a quick look at the screen, she grinned at him. "I'll have to remember that you can be as literal as Ian. I was telling *you* I'd be back in a few minutes. Do you have a spare house key hidden somewhere outside, like under a flowerpot or a rock?"

Hadn't Chloe told him about an extra key in case he got locked out?

Key. Door. Lock. Water. "The underside of the bird bath."

"Good. Do you mind if my mom goes into the house and cleans up the water? Getting the floors dry is kind of important. I can fix the faucet later."

He typed "mother hen" into the search bar on his phone and clicked on the first result. "Mother hen. Don't you like that she wants to help?"

"Aw, I just like to tease her. She'd do anything for me, day or night, including helping me with a plumbing job. Are you okay with letting her into your house while you're not there?"

Despite the fact that he'd lived there for more than two months, he still thought of the house as Chloe's. "I think so."

Her thumbs popped back and forth, presumably in answer to her mom's response. Then she handed him her phone and started the engine. "I asked her to wipe down the bathroom and get as much water as she can from the carpet. Knowing her, she'll take home all the towels and wash them for me, too."

"Oh, thanks for lunch. Sometimes I forget to say it. I'll have the apple juice." He double-checked his seat belt as she backed out of the space. "Should I pay your mom for helping or is that included in what I owe you?"

"No charge."

"But you—"

"Elijah Clayton, you're giving me something more precious than I ever imagined." Her eyes shifted toward him for a second. "Besides, I can't charge my husband for a plumbing job in the house where we'll be living together. As for Mom, we'll settle up with her in a few days."

Was she referring to Eve? After having her own baby die and no possibility of having another, she might consider Eve precious. "We aren't married yet."

"Close enough. Go ahead and eat. I had breakfast. You didn't." With her gaze aimed forward, she laughed. "You realize my mom is going to be your mother-in-law, don't you?"

He stopped in the middle of unwrapping his sandwich. "Is that good or bad?"

The turn signal clicked as she changed lanes and then went silent again. "Good, as long as she likes you, but I don't think you have anything to worry about. She's getting a son-in-law and another grandchild in one fell swoop."

"What if she thinks I'm weird?" The scent of roast beef and Swiss made his stomach growl.

"Everybody's weird, at least in my family. You'll fit right in." She glanced at him again, her smile gone. "You know I'm just joking with you, don't you? It's easier than thinking about why we're getting married."

"I didn't think you were trying to be mean. I *am* weird sometimes." Since her expression didn't change, he could only guess that the terrible reality he'd accepted over the last seven weeks was finally sinking in. "Chloe told me I'm only allowed to be sad for a little while after she dies. She wants Eve to grow up with happy memories of her, not wondering if her mom would've lived if she hadn't been pregnant. Eve is a miracle."

"She is, but it's still not fair." Beatrix's whisper barely carried to his ears over the engine and road noises.

Determined not to jump to conclusions about her meaning, he bit into his sandwich. Life wasn't always fair, and his cousin had assured him that Eve was lucky to have him. Chloe wouldn't have encouraged Beatrix to hold and nurse the baby if she didn't believe it was best for all of them.

Beatrix was quiet as she navigated through downtown traffic, seeming to know exactly where to turn and which streets went which direction. A right turn took them into a parking garage. "We'll park here and walk. It's quicker than trying to find a metered spot on the street."

"Okay. Do you know where we're supposed to go?" He shoved the last bite of sandwich in his mouth.

"Yep." A frown replaced her unreadable face. "You didn't have to eat so fast. I wouldn't have taken it from you."

He crumpled the wrapper and stuffed it in the bag. "But it gets cold if I eat it too slowly."

Her snort suggested she was annoyed with him. "Something else you have in common with my nephew. Only unwrap the part you're biting. Then the rest stays warm longer and you can actually enjoy it. Ugh. Why can't people park straight?"

Fairly certain her question was rhetorical, he smothered the urge to offer an explanation and took a long drink of juice. Their marriage would probably be a lot more pleasant if he censored his thoughts before they came out his mouth.

She finally pulled into a space on the third level. "Ready?"

With a nod, he grabbed the bag with her lunch and climbed out of the truck. Since she would need both hands to eat her sandwich, walking beside her seemed like a better choice than holding her hand, even if he did like the comfortable feel of her fingers clasped between his. "Which way?"

"To the skywalk." She set off at a brisk pace. "You don't get out much, do you?"

Speeding up to keep pace with her, he walked with her across the nearly full lot. "I go to work every day. Well, Monday through Friday. And I drive to the hospital and the grocery store. Where else would I go? Besides the dating events, I mean. I don't need to do that anymore."

"Nope. I sure won't miss those."

He handed her the bag as they entered the walkway over the street. "You should eat while we walk to the courthouse."

She smiled when their hands touched. "Mm-hm. Thanks."

Matching her step for step, he patted his back pocket to make sure he hadn't forgotten his wallet. The dollar bills she'd tossed onto the table at the coffee shop popped into his thoughts when he made contact with the bump of folded leather. "Beatrix, would you have gone out with me if we'd met under different circumstances?"

She slid the sandwich from the bag, not slowing her pace. "Does it matter? I've learned a lot from what I've been through. Looking back means you aren't looking forward. How about we forget about what brought us together and concentrate on the future?"

CHAPTER EIGHT

STILL SHOCKED BY HOW MUCH SENSE HER EARLIER LOGIC MADE, Beatrix handed Judge Bradley the marriage license and accepted that fate probably knew better than she did, at least where men were concerned. “We really appreciate you taking time out of your schedule to perform the ceremony, Your Honor.”

The gray-haired man glanced across the hall toward Chloe’s room and back again. “I’d do damn near anything to make sure that little girl has some happiness in her life. Did you know her daddy died saving my son and two other men in their fire crew?”

She shook her head and prayed she didn’t bawl her eyes out at the loss Eve would never remember enduring. “No, Chloe and Elijah didn’t tell me how he died.”

“He was braver than most people could ever imagine being.” Judge Bradley looked down toward the paper she’d handed him, as if to make sure everything was in order. “The same goes for his wife.”

The door across the hall opened and Mrs. Long exited. She gave Beatrix a brief hug, the lines on her face more visible than when she’d arrived. “Thanks for the coffee. I’m going to go for a walk. It’s so hard to see her like this. I’ll be back in a little bit.”

Glad she'd cut Eve's grandmother some slack, Beatrix smiled. "Take as much time as you need. And thanks for staying."

The older woman nodded and hurried toward the elevators.

Judge Bradley tapped the paper against his palm. "Looks like we're ready."

Beatrix followed him into Chloe's room, certain she'd made the only decision she could, even if Brian's mom probably wouldn't contest the will or the custody arrangements. The timing of the wedding was irrelevant—today or two weeks from now—and explaining the situation to her family would be far less difficult if the deed was already done.

The nurse adjusted Chloe's arm to cradle Eve, but her patient didn't seem aware of the movement. Only a noisy breath and a twitch of her right eyelid suggested she was still alive.

Eli's gaze met Beatrix's from his cousin's bedside, the emotion in his eyes triggering another urge to cry. "We need to hurry. It's happening too fast. She doesn't have much time left."

Joining her husband-to-be, Beatrix grasped his hand. Its chill was evidence of the distress he had to be feeling. "Everybody's here. Are you sure you want to get married?"

He tightened his hold on her fingers. "Yes. I can't do this alone."

A tiny stab of hurt tried to convince her to rethink her choice. He might not be able to express his thoughts in the most sensitive way, but his heart was in the right place. An admission of helplessness had to mean he trusted her. She would have to remember not to read too much into his blunt responses. He likely couldn't pull off pretense if he wanted to. Alone obviously meant without her—watching Chloe fade away and parenting Eve.

She kissed his cheek, at least a day's worth of stubble tickling her chin. "You're not alone, Elijah. I'm right here."

"Thank you." His voice broke slightly over the words.

John Lathrop stepped closer to the bed, his solemn expression more suited to a funeral than a birth or a wedding. "Since everyone's present, why don't we go ahead with the ceremony?"

As he opened a small book, Judge Bradley cleared his throat.

"Friends and loved ones, we are gathered here to witness the joining of Elijah Clayton and Beatrix Glouster in marriage. Their life together is just beginning and the commitment they have to one another will give them strength along their journey. Lead with your hearts, Elijah and Beatrix. Support and guide each other through the days, months, and years ahead, knowing that together you are stronger."

Eve's soft coo contrasted with another of her mother's rattling breaths, and Eli's grasp tightened again.

The judge turned the page. "Do you, Elijah, take Beatrix as your wife, through joyous and troubling times, for as long as you both shall live?"

"I do." Though barely audible, his promise sounded confident and sincere.

"Do you, Beatrix, take Elijah as your husband, through joyous and troubling times, for as long as you both shall live?"

We're off to rough start.

A hot tear escaped, and she let it roll to the corner of her mouth. She'd give her all to make this marriage last. "I do."

With a ribbon marking his place, Judge closed his book. "Will you be exchanging rings?"

Eli groaned and dropped his chin to his chest. "I didn't think of those. I'm sorry."

The lawyer reached over the bed. "I knew you wouldn't have time to buy rings, so I picked up a couple on my way back to the office. My wedding gift."

Grateful for the older man's thoughtfulness and generosity, Beatrix took the small blue box. A pair of plain gold bands glinted in the dim lighting. "Thanks, Mr. Lathrop. We really appreciate it. Take the smaller one, Eli. It's okay. I didn't think of them, either."

Eli's dark waves dipped across his forehead as he lifted his head, making him look much younger than mid-thirtyish. "What if it doesn't fit?"

"Then we'll have it resized." She released his hand and slid the rings from the velvet lining. "Here."

Obviously accustomed to awkward interruptions during his officiating, Judge Bradley reopened his book. "These rings are a symbol of your promises to each other and the life you will share. Elijah, please place the ring on Beatrix's finger and repeat after me. With this ring, I pledge myself to you."

The band slipped over her knuckle, its fit snug but comfortable. "With this ring, I pledge myself to you."

"And, Beatrix, please place the ring on Elijah's finger and repeat after me. With this ring, I pledge myself to you."

She eased the band past the tip of his finger, praying it gave Eli no reason to doubt the decision they'd made. A firm push helped it slide into place. *Thank you!* "With this ring, I pledge myself to you."

"By the authority vested in me by the State of Ohio, I now pronounce you husband and wife. I highly recommend a kiss to celebrate this wonderful occasion, Mr. and Mrs. Clayton."

Eli wrapped his arm around her waist and lowered his mouth to hers. Warmth surrounded her as his tongue snuck past her lips. Each tentative glide hinted at something more, promising a wedding night she would remember forever. She clung to him to keep from melting to the floor, but all too soon his mouth was gone, unlike the desire thrumming through her body. Their marriage promised to be an interesting ride if he surprised her with kisses like those often.

John Lathrop caressed the baby's downy head. He repeated the tender gesture with her mother. "Congratulations, Eli. Beatrix. May you have many happy years together. It's done, Chloe. Your mom and dad will be here soon and you'll be able to rest."

He murmured something to the judge, and they walked out of the room together.

The nurse lifted Eve from the bed. "That was my first hospital wedding. Yours too, I suspect, little one. It's almost feeding time. Eli, why don't you change her diaper while I help Beatrix get set up."

Wide-eyed, he followed her to the sink. "I don't know how to change a diaper."

"Wash up first. Then I'll talk you through it while we prepare the formula and tubing. The important thing to remember is babies can't control when they need to potty, so you're going to want to get done fast and keep things covered." She pointed to the storage areas below the tiny bed. "Diaper and wipes. Have those ready before you start."

She continued her verbal instructions as Beatrix tried to focus on her task instead of watching Eli's expression go from discomfort to trepidation. As uncomfortable as he'd been simply holding Eve, he had to be terrified by the thought of changing a diaper. What if he was a germophobe like Ian?

An angry cry tore her attention from the pouch of formula.

Eli cringed, but the sound of the tape peeling from the diaper competed with unhappy wailing. "You're right, Eve. I'm not good at this, but I'll try to learn."

The fussing paused for a moment before starting up again.

With the tubing now attached to the pouch, Beatrix double-checked the connection for leaks. "I told you she likes hearing your voice. Maybe you need to talk to her to keep her from crying."

"What should I talk about?"

She shrugged. "I don't know. You're a poet. Make up a silly rhyme."

His eyebrows dipped toward the bridge of his nose. "Poetry is more than silly rhymes."

A laugh almost escaped at his affronted tone and the ease with which she'd managed to distract him. "Then prove it."

He cleared his throat. "'I hear your heartbeat, though you've yet to take a breath. I trace your delicate features, but I've yet to touch you. I watch your tiny feet run without meeting the ground, and I feel joy in my soul at the miracle you are. Will I smell the sweet scent of your newborn skin? Will I hold my perfect angel in my arms? I will gladly give you life in exchange for wings and I will watch over you until the end of time.'" He fastened the second side of the clean diaper and glanced toward the hospital bed. "I wrote that poem about you and your mom, Eve. She asked me to go with her to the last ultrasound. Those are the things I saw."

Agony ripped through Beatrix's middle. For a man who couldn't speak with any sense of tact at times, he had a remarkable talent for putting her in her place with his words. She'd had those same thoughts about her own unborn child only days before the unthinkable had happened. Given a choice, she would've gladly exchanged her life for wings and an eternity of watching over the baby on the monitor.

The knot in her stomach clamped tighter, setting off a wave of nausea. She gripped the back of the chair and closed her eyes against the onslaught of grief and regret. Time hadn't healed the invisible wounds. Only the physical scars had faded.

I can't do this.

Pretending to be a mother wouldn't bring back her son, and Eli was no more her husband than Derek had been. She was a means to an end again.

What have I done?

"Mrs. Clayton, are you all right?" The nurse turned toward her. "You look awfully pale. Beatrix?"

Beatrix spun the meaningless ring on her finger.

I made a mistake. A huge mistake.

She pushed past the nurse, the need to escape guiding her toward the hallway. Fingers closed around her upper arm, adding to the drag of her heavy legs, but she twisted away. How could she have married a man who had the power to slice her heart to shreds with a few words?

Again.

The door handle blurred as she reached for it. Thankfully, a blind grab yielded cold metal. The handle moved, but the door didn't open.

"The poem. I didn't think." Eli's arms closed around her from behind, his body forming a cocoon against her back and shoulders. "Don't go. I didn't mean to upset you."

The will to fight gave way to familiar pain. Tears came easier than a battle, not that she had any idea how to banish the soul-deep ache.

It isn't supposed to hurt like this anymore.

His beard-roughened jaw brushed her cheek as he curled tighter around her. "I don't know what to do. The poem was for Chloe and Eve. It wasn't supposed to hurt you." He rested his head against hers.

"I'm sorry. You have every right to go, but I can't do this without you. I *need* you. Will you stay? Please."

The gentle sincerity in his softly spoken words calmed the panic and soothed the pain more than anything her family had said or done. He was practically a total stranger. How could he incite so many emotions and reactions within her?

Am I strong enough to stay?

A call to the judge could prevent him from filing the marriage license. She wouldn't be obligated to put her heart on the line, with Eli or the baby. She would also give up what might be her only chance to be a mother.

Can I leave without regrets?

"Please say something." The desperation in his voice went far beyond that of his plumbing message on her answering machine.

How many times had she wished for Derek to console her instead of adding to the already overwhelming guilt her defective body had caused? Only months of anger had finally gotten her through his lack of support and desertion. It had been effortless compared to grieving.

She squeezed her eyes shut to stem the flow of tears. "It's not your fault."

"It must be. I made you cry."

She ached to lean into him, to let his touch ground her. "My past, not you."

"But I made you remember."

"I'll never forget, even if I choose not to think about it." That single truth would always haunt her. "You need someone who isn't damaged."

"If you're damaged, what am I?" He turned her around in his arms and lifted her palm to his damp cheek. "I can't watch you cry without crying myself. We belong together. Chloe knew it as soon as she met you. And I'm not letting you go."

The stubborn jut of his jaw matched Ian's when her nephew took a stand. Nothing anyone did or said could change his mind.

She leaned her forehead against his chest, too stunned to argue his territorial statement. *He's willing to fight for me.* "Okay."

"You'll stay?"

Comforted by the hope in his question, she lifted her head and nodded. "I promise I'm not usually this emotional."

"I'm not, either. It's been a hard day. I don't think I could've handled most of it if you hadn't been here."

"I'm sorry—for what you're going through and the meltdown." A knock on the door interrupted the much-needed cuddle she wanted to share with him. "What now?"

His sigh expressed every bit of her frustration. "I'll see who's there."

She settled for an abbreviated hug and then she headed into the bathroom. Puffy eyes and a tear-stained face greeted her in the mirror. At least she'd washed off last night's mascara before she'd gone to bed. A few splashes of cool water cleared some of the blotchiness, but even blowing her nose several times didn't make breathing through her nose any easier. If Eli refused to let her go after an ugly-cry, he was even less shallow than she gave him credit for.

He doesn't know how to be shallow. I can take every word and action at face value.

After a few deep breaths, she marched out of the bathroom, determined to put the past behind her and focus on the new man in her life and the child they would raise together.

Low voices carried to the doorway, but a tiny wail called to her above the soft murmurs.

I'm so sorry for thinking I could leave you, Eve. Never again. I promise.

A man and woman stood at Chloe's bedside, grief written in their expressions. Another couple followed Eli to the bassinet. The similarities in his and the second man's features made their connection obvious.

Elijah's jaw flexed and he gestured for her to join them. "Beatrix, meet my parents."

My new in-laws.

She cursed the sudden dryness in her throat and tried for her best smile. "Nice to meet you, Mr. and Mrs. Clayton."

Their eyebrows rose in unison, suggesting that an introduction to a woman by their son wasn't commonplace or quite what they'd expected.

"Mom. Dad. This is Beatrix. My wife."

Mrs. Clayton's mouth opened and closed twice. "*Wife?*"

CHAPTER NINE

Leaving Beatrix to nurse Eve in relative privacy and his aunt and uncle at Chloe's bedside, Eli led his parents to the waiting area across the hall. Subtlety had never been one of his better social skills, and he'd most certainly failed again, given his mom's repetition of the word "wife" and his dad's deep frown. The look they exchanged as they sat on the couch confirmed his suspicions.

A rumbling growl came from his stomach, but suggesting they go have supper would only delay the conversation.

His mom glanced toward Chloe's room and back again. "Why didn't you tell us you were getting married?"

"We decided at the last minute." Every inch of him itched, but he tucked his hands under his legs instead of picking at his fingernails or scratching his forearms until his skin burned.

His dad stared at him for what seemed like an hour. "You were in that much of a rush that you couldn't call us? Is she pregnant?"

Heat flooded Eli's neck and ears. "We…but… She isn't pregnant. Brian's mom thought she should get custody of Eve, and Mr. Lathrop said the guardianship was less likely to be challenged if we were married."

"Who's Mr. Lathrop?" The familiar critical expression warned him that his dad hadn't gotten past the disapproving mindset he'd had for much of Eli's adult life. "You'd better start at the beginning, because I don't understand why you couldn't have at least told us you were involved in a serious relationship. This had to have been going on for a while if you were thinking about marriage."

Unable to hold his father's steady gaze, Eli focused on the dark blue line running the length of the carpet and lined up the toes of his shoes against it. "Chloe found out she had the tumor right after I moved here. She asked me to become Eve's legal guardian. I knew I wouldn't be able to do it by myself, so she helped me sign up for some dating services. I met Beatrix and she came with me to the hospital. Chloe said we were perfect for each other. Everything happened really fast. Mr. Lathrop is her lawyer."

His dad's noisy exhale warned him the interrogation wasn't over. "How fast? Chloe met her?"

Eli nodded without looking up, hoping to get by without answering the first question.

His mom patted his knee. "If Chloe approves of this Beatrix, then she must be a nice girl. You know we're just worried about you, don't you? Does she make you happy?"

A slight adjustment put his feet in line with the gray stripe. "We're still getting to know each other, but I like her. She understands me better than most people."

"I'm so thrilled to hear that. And she doesn't mind raising Chloe's baby?"

"No." He adjusted his feet again, this time lining them up with the purple stripe. "She didn't think she'd ever be a mother. When she was married before, she had a baby and it died."

"Oh my! That poor young woman."

"She was married before?" His dad pushed up from the couch. "And the baby died? What have you gotten yourself into?"

His mom tsked. "I think our son deserves the benefit of the doubt. You don't even know Beatrix, and you've already decided she's the worst thing that's ever happened to him."

"And how do you know she didn't marry him for dishonest

reasons? He isn't exactly the best judge of character. Chloe's bound to have life insurance, besides the house and whatever money she has left from Brian's policy."

The critical tone in his dad's voice pushed Eli's nerves closer to the edge, making him wish he could disappear. He scooted forward on his seat, ready for a quick exit. "If nobody had ulterior motives, I wouldn't have to judge anybody's character. Maybe you should blame the people who are jerks instead of the people who think everybody should be nice. Beatrix is nice and I'm glad I married her."

Silence stretched forever before his dad sat. "It's probably too late to annul the marriage anyway."

"Annulment?" His mom frowned. "What a horrible thing to say."

Eli tried unsuccessfully to relax the muscles in his neck and jaw. He should've been used to having his decisions second-guessed, but it still stung. How could his dad care more about why he chose to marry Beatrix than the fact that Chloe was dying?

The ache in his stomach sharpened. "I have to…to…have to…to be there… Damn it. I have to be there for Chloe and Eve and Beatrix."

He hurried from the waiting area before his dad could chastise him for swearing, on top of everything else. His reasons for moving halfway across the country, first for grad school and then for a job, came to the forefront again. Praise for good grades didn't cancel out the lack of confidence in his decision-making skills.

I made the right choice this time. I know I did.

The door eased open with a gentle push.

His aunt and uncle still stood at Chloe's bedside. They looked at him as he entered the room, but he wasn't up to joining them for a vigil over his dying cousin. Watching her body fail had been difficult enough when she'd been conscious. He no longer had the strength to witness the remainder of life draining from the vibrant woman he'd once known. The part he would miss was already gone and the rest would soon follow.

As he passed the bassinet, Beatrix adjusted the blanket draped over shoulder, hiding both her breast and Eve from view. "You look upset. Is everything okay?"

With a shrug, he sat in the chair beside her. "My dad took the news about as well as I expected. You don't think we made a mistake, do you?"

"You're asking me, after the meltdown I had? I have no idea." She glanced at him and then down toward the bundle in her arms. "It's what Chloe wants, so I think we need to trust that she knows what's best for her baby. This is going to be hard for both of us, and I can't guarantee I won't flip out again, but I'll do my best to make it work if you will."

The alternative wasn't something he even wanted to imagine—living without the one person besides his cousin who seemed to understand him, raising Eve by himself, and proving his dad right—that he wasn't capable of making a decision on his own. "I want us to have a good marriage. Will your mom and dad be mad?"

"Mad? No, but they might question my sanity if I don't tell them the whole story. Even then, they might. I'm usually the levelheaded one."

The blanket slipped down her arm, revealing a narrow strip of bare skin above the baby's head. Overanalyzing her statement seemed wiser than giving in to the urge to stare at his wife's soft curves. "Marriages based on rational reasons have a lower than average divorce rate. Isn't that levelheaded?"

"Maybe to you and me, but my family is going to think I'm off my rocker." She tugged at the cover and licked her lips. "Time to switch sides. You should probably turn around or something. I haven't quite mastered the art of rearranging Eve, the tubing, *and* my clothes."

He pivoted the chair toward the far wall and sat again. "Do you want me to ask the lactation consultant to come back?"

"No, thanks. I need to figure out how to do it by myself. Unless the pediatrician finds a problem, Eve will be going home in a day or two and we'll be on our own, at least for the most part. Speaking of home, do you have a supply of diapers and wipes at the house? Maybe we should pick up some supplies when we get supper. Oh, and formula. Probably at least three or four days' worth."

The rustle of clothing tempted him to look back at her, but he pulled his phone from his pocket to check his email instead. "Chloe stocked the nursery with everything I'd need for the first couple weeks. Diapers, clothes, blankets, formula. She put a list on top of the dresser."

"Okay."

He turned toward her at the verbal indication that she'd finished rearranging the baby. The sooner he learned to read some of her facial expressions, the better.

A pair of taut nipples stared back at him. "Not yet! I meant okay to the list, not that I was done."

Heat rushed to his cheeks at her hissed scolding, but he couldn't force his eyes from her breasts. The strip of cloth tape and the plastic tube triggered a more basic feeling than simple sexual attraction. It was unfamiliar, but the tightness in his chest brought calm rather than panic.

He lifted Eve from the makeshift cradle of Beatrix's crossed legs. "I'll hold her until you're ready."

"You didn't have to do that. I know how uncomfortable all of this makes you."

"I'm not uncomfortable with you or the baby. Just nervous." As he touched Eve's tiny hand, she wrapped her fingers around his thumb, squeezing tighter than he would've thought possible. "She's so strong, like Chloe and you."

"You're just as strong. Look at everything you've done for them. Most men would've run the other direction at the prospect of becoming a husband and father this way. You're also the most loyal person I've ever met." Beatrix bit her lower lip and tore off the overlapping tape holding the tubing in place.

He flinched at the faint ripping sound and shivered at the ripple of sympathetic pain on his skin.

"You look kind of pale. You're not going to faint, are you?"

The room swayed a little, but he shook his head. "No, but that had to hurt. Do you need some lotion or ointment or something? I can check with the nurse."

"It only stings for a few seconds. Besides, I'm tough." She repositioned the tube along the side of her other breast and taped it in place. "Okay, let's see how I did."

Placing Eve in her arms, he made no attempt to avoid touching Beatrix. Every tiny connection to her convinced him he was almost normal. The baby latched on as if she knew exactly what to do. "It looks like you don't need me."

"Maybe not, but I'm glad you were here just in case." With the blanket draped over her shoulder again, she looked up at him. "I don't feel so lost and alone in some bizarre dream. It makes me like you even more."

The giddy sensation in his belly was probably a good sign. "I like you too."

As he moved his chair closer to her, his parents came into the room. Eli ran his palm along the length of his wife's ponytail as he sat, unwilling to let his dad's disapproval ruin the important moment they'd shared. The way she leaned into his touch assured him that, somehow, they would make their marriage work and give Eve the loving home she deserved.

He tried to tune out the low murmur of voices at Chloe's bedside, but Mrs. Long's return prompted a constant exchange of words, making him wish he could go home. Chloe had warned him the end would mean no more quiet visitation with the two of them reading together and sharing memories. She'd tried to prepare him, despite his shortcomings.

He propped his elbows on his knees and rested his head in his hands. The position allowed him to cover his ears with his thumbs, blocking out some of the unwanted conversation without anyone being the wiser.

The oncologist's noiseless entrance a few minutes later brought utter silence, with the exception of Chloe's rattling breaths. The sound reminded him of the timeline the doctor had given him after he'd mentioned how confusing all the online information had been.

It's almost time.

How had it happened so fast?

Beatrix touched her fingertips to his cheek, wiping away a tear that had leaked from the corner of his eye. Her soft voice near his ear soothed some of the sadness spreading through him. "Are you okay? Eve's almost done. We can go for a walk if you want to."

A nod was all he could manage. His cousin had promised to be there as long as he needed her, but now he had someone new to depend on. Somehow she'd fought for her life until he had found Beatrix. He'd never be able to repay her for that, even by giving her daughter a family. Chloe and Brian would've been better parents than he could ever aspire to be. All he could hope for was that, with his wife's help, he didn't screw up too badly.

"Come on. The tubing can soak while we're gone." Beatrix stood, first touching her lips to Eve's forehead and then lowering her into the bassinet. She feathered her fingertips along the curve of the baby's ear, much the same as his cousin had done on the ultrasound screen. "She'll probably sleep for at least an hour."

After a stop at the sink, he followed his wife into the hallway, thankful to find it empty of its usual afternoon activity. Each step brought a small measure of relief, like the feel of her fingers laced through his. The elevator doors whooshed closed behind them.

His neck muscles finally unclenched. "Did you get to hold your baby?"

"Only for a few seconds." Her words came out on a near whisper. "He'd already died by the time the doctor delivered him and then...the complications. They had to put me under to save my life. For a while, I wished I'd died with him."

"I'm glad the doctor saved you."

"You're a better man than my ex-husband. Derek said it was my fault his son died, that it should've been me instead." The doors opened at the ground floor and she walked with him toward the exit. "Let's go outside."

"People say mean things without thinking." The smell of car exhaust greeted him as they left the building, but it was a pleasant change from the antiseptic odor of the hospital. "My dad thinks I made a bad decision by marrying you."

She guided him toward the street. "What *you* think is more important since you have to live with your decision. It's your mistake to make."

"Or not make. I'm not a kid anymore." Exhaustion slowed his pace, and she adjusted her speed to match his instead of forcing him to keep up with her. "I don't want to be there when Chloe dies."

A gentle squeeze of his hand accompanied Beatrix's sniffle. "And that's okay. I'm sure she understands."

"But nobody else will."

"I do." She bumped her shoulder against his. "I'm guessing you've said your goodbyes to her, probably a hundred times. She seems ready to go. Being with her won't change that."

"It doesn't feel like she's here anymore." He stopped at a bus-stop bench, too weary to move another inch. "Do you mind if we sit for a while?"

"Whatever you need." Without letting go of his hand, she brushed away the fallen leaves and then sat beside him. "Maybe she was just waiting to hold Eve and make sure you're not alone. She wouldn't go if she didn't think you were ready."

"I wouldn't be ready without you. Thank you." That admission was the absolute truth. He wouldn't have survived the day without the woman he'd known only as Beatrix-35 yesterday. How had so much happened in so little time?

"You're welcome." She nestled closer, her leg touching him from hip to ankle and her head resting on his shoulder. "Close your eyes and take a deep breath."

The soothing scent of her hair replaced the smell of cars. *Chai latté.*

She snuggled even closer. "Good. And a slow exhale."

The tension dissipated from his muscles, leaving only his usual superficial worries. He could deal with those. The rest he let go, trusting that his cousin knew him better than he knew himself. He drew in another breath. This one smelled of amaretto cookies. As he released it, a sense of peace washed over him.

"Eli, your phone's vibrating against my leg." The urgency in Beatrix's voice pulled him from the edge of sleep. "Eli."

He blinked away his bleary vision, but his mind had already cleared. "She's gone."

CHAPTER TEN

"We'll take extra good care of her." The nurse gave Beatrix's arm a gentle pat to accompany her kind smile. "Go home and get some rest."

If not for the utter exhaustion and grief carved on Eli's face, Beatrix would've planted her feet and refused to leave. Instead, she leaned over the bassinet and pressed her lips to the baby's forehead. "Sleep well, Eve. We'll be back in the morning."

Before her willpower abandoned her, she grasped her husband's hand and walked along the quiet corridor. He needed her more than their child did right now.

"Do you mind if we take the stairs?" He pointed toward a lighted sign past the elevators. "I don't want to be around people, especially my family. All the emotional noise is too much."

Giving a nod, she ignored the implication that he wanted to be alone. He didn't, even if he hadn't voiced his wish for her to stay with him. They were a single unit now, and getting used to his way of thinking was surprisingly easy. She'd never have to read between the lines for disguised insults and judgments like she had with her ex near the end of their marriage.

Maybe Elijah isn't perfect, but I don't have to be, either.

He pushed the door open and held it until she stepped into the stairwell. Their footsteps echoed through empty space, but his voice was low. “I have to meet with the funeral director tomorrow. There are a couple things we couldn’t finish until after Chloe died.”

Despite the evenness of the words, his palpable dread crept up her spine. “I have to feed Eve first thing in the morning, but I can go with you after that.”

“You don’t have to if you don’t want to.”

“I wouldn’t have offered if I didn’t want to.” She turned toward him on the landing two floors above the lobby level. “It isn’t a pleasant job, but we’re going to do it together because we take care of each other now. For better or worse. You stood up to your parents on my behalf. I’ll be with you to handle Chloe’s final arrangements.”

“Okay.” Lines etched his forehead for a long moment before he leaned in and kissed her on the cheek. “Thank you.”

“You’re welcome.” She touched her fingertip to the spot, surprised by the simple joy his show of appreciation brought. “That was nice.”

“I’m glad you liked it. I wasn’t sure it was the right thing to do.” He edged toward the next flight of stairs. “I wanted to do it earlier at your house, but I was worried about… I guess I didn’t want to do the wrong thing.”

“You’re a better man than most for admitting it.” After a quick brush of her mouth on his, she led him down the stairs. “For the record, I trust your instincts when it comes to kissing me. You should too.”

His hold on her hand tightened slightly, but he was silent the rest of the walk to her truck and the drive to her condo.

As she shut off the engine in front of the garage, he rubbed his hands down his pant legs. Then he blew out a noisy breath. “Are we staying here tonight?”

The uncertainty in his voice confirmed her suspicions about the sudden attack of nervousness. “No, you’ve had enough disruptions in your routine for one day. I’m just picking up a few changes of clothes and a toothbrush before we head to your house. I’ll be gone five minutes, tops. You can wait here if you want.”

He cleared his throat. “Yeah, I better stay in your truck.”

The security light above the garage door illuminated enough of the bulge in his pants to give away his reason for not going with her. An unexpected contraction pulsed through her vaginal muscles at his obvious sexual interest. She had to agree with his probable reasoning. They likely wouldn't make it out of her bedroom until morning if he accompanied her.

You're a lot more normal than you think, Eli Clayton.

"Be back shortly." She hurried inside, determined not to add to his anxiety.

The message light on her business line blinked in the kitchen, but she climbed the stairs two at a time instead of wasting time. Her personal life took priority right now. Any of the dozens of other plumbers in the area could handle the workload while she adapted to being a wife and mother.

Married again. And finally a mother. Is this even real?

She paused with the bathroom drawer halfway open to stare back at the woman in the mirror. How had her life changed so completely in such a short time? Would she wake up from the crazy dream and have to accept another loss that would hurt every bit as much as the last one?

The ring on her finger was proof enough to spur her into packing an overnight bag. She shoved her travel kit into the tote and returned to the bedroom for several changes of clothes. Button-down shirts seemed easiest to manage with the supplemental feeding system she'd have to use until her body produced the nourishment Eve needed, and jeans would suffice for whatever life had in store for her tomorrow.

Socks and undies.

Peacock-green lace peeked out from under the pile of bikini briefs as she added bras and underwear to her bag. She had set aside the birthday gift she'd given herself over a year ago at least a dozen times, in case she met someone worthy of seeing her in it. The thigh-length nightie unfolded when she pulled it free, lace-trimmed silk landing on top of the socks she'd packed.

Elijah is worthy, and it's our wedding night. She pushed her surprise to the bottom of the bag and closed the drawer with her hip. *Done.*

She scuttled down the stairs, fairly certain he was counting the milliseconds until her return. What man with a hard-on wouldn't?

His shaky sigh as she slid behind wheel confirmed her suspicions. "How'd I do?"

"Four minutes and fifty-three seconds." He hooked his hand behind her neck and closed the space between them. After a tentative peck on the mouth, he made contact again, this time gliding his tongue along the seam of her lips.

She let him inside, wallowing in the melty sensation his kiss triggered. Each gentle meeting of tongues, combined with his soft hums vibrating through her jaw, amplified the need to consummate their marriage. His unhurried exit left her winded and wishing she hadn't promised to drive another ten minutes to his house.

He rested his forehead against hers, his panting breaths tickling her nose. "Wow. Can we go home now?"

"Mm-hm. Where'd you learn to kiss like that?"

"I Googled it while you were gone."

"Excellent use of your time." She slid her palm up his thigh and cupped his erection. It pulsed and grew against her fingers. "Buckle up."

His groan suggested he would've preferred unbuckling, but he followed her instructions as she started the engine. "I've never been to this part of town. How far is it to Chloe's house?"

"Less than five miles." Stretching her arm across the back of his seat, she turned to look out the rear window as she backed out of the driveway. The urge to trace the curve of his jaw proved too strong. "What other topics did you Google?"

He jumped at the contact. "Oh, um, just some…some…other stuff related to, um, sex."

Only her hurry to get to his house kept her from slamming on the brakes in the middle of the road and giving him her full attention. "What kind of stuff?"

His half cough, half choke might have made her laugh if she wasn't so damn curious. "Hm. Um, what women like."

"You know not all women like the same things during sex, don't you? Personally, I enjoy oral sex as foreplay. Giving and receiving."

A strangled squeak came from the passenger side. "But there are *germs* on—"

"Door knobs, hands, grocery carts. Pretty much everything. I can take a shower first if it'll squick you out less." She accelerated through a yellow light. "Or we can take a shower together."

"But…" A streetlight illuminated his wide eyes.

"We'll go slow at first. Experiment. See what you like and don't like." She grinned at him. "You might actually enjoy going down on me."

"Cunnilingus."

"Yes." The turn signal clicked off as she turned onto his street. "And fellatio is the same as a blow job. And before you ask, a blow job is more 'thar she blows!' like a spouting whale than blowing. It's mostly licking and sucking. We're here."

His moan sounded more pained than the squeak. "Interesting analogy for the male orgasm, although whales expel air, not liquid. Unfortunately, I don't know if I can walk."

She shut off the engine and aimed a wicked smile at him. "You want to have sex in my truck instead of your bed?"

"No!" The horrified look on his face answered her question as loud and clear as his denial. He unbuckled his seatbelt and reached toward the door handle. "People might see us. I think I can make it."

"Do you need help getting your keys out of your pocket? I'll be happy to—"

"I can do it." He opened the door and climbed out. "Let's go inside."

"Party pooper." She slung her bag over her shoulder and followed him to the front porch, glad to have taken his mind off the harshness life had dealt him today.

"Parties make me nervous. Too many people, and usually there's alcohol. I don't drink." A sliver of light shone across the entry floor, but he didn't enter. "I didn't leave the kitchen light on."

"My mom probably turned it on before she left. We should go see what I need to do, besides replacing the faucet." She led him into the house and closed the door. "Lock up while I check the damage."

Without a backward glance, she retraced her earlier steps from the entry to the master bedroom, flipping on the hall light when she passed the switch. The nursery tempted her to stop for a closer look, but she continued past it to her new bedroom.

A swath of light from the hall led her to the bed, still unmade—with packaged faucets and an unopened condom resting on the crumpled covers. The low hum of a fan came from the shadows near the bathroom, but the wet vac and duffle bag of work towels were gone. Stacks of clean bath towels filled the shelving opposite the toilet.

She plopped her overnight bag on the floor and turned on the bedside lamp before focusing her attention on the reason she'd made her early-morning house call. The vanity cabinet was wide open, presumably to dry, and the floor no longer doubled as a wading pool. A tented note stood on the counter.

"Trixie, I took your towels home to wash. Your tools and supplies are where you left them, except the vac. I'll drop that off at your house on the way home. I put the key back under the birdbath. Let me know if you need anything else. Love you! Mom"

"Bless you, Mom."

"It looks dry." Eli touched his fingertip to the wall beside her.

"It is. Your mother-in-law is an amazing woman. Why don't you take a shower while I replace the faucet and make arrangements for a family meeting tomorrow evening? The sooner Mom and Dad meet you and Eve, the better."

His eyebrows dipped toward his nose. "You're going to be in the bathroom at the same time I'm in the shower?"

"Well, yeah. It's not like you'll be on the toilet—which is *not* part of sharing a bathroom, by the way. Door closed during and lid down after. Agreed?"

Every muscle in his face unclenched with her mandate. "Agreed. I don't go in public restrooms unless I absolutely have to. I never liked locker rooms, either, but seeing you naked is acceptable."

"Acceptable, huh?" Her hoot of laughter was loud in the small space. "I'm pretty sure you find it more than just acceptable."

His gaze slid toward her breasts and a hint of a smile curved his lips. "Okay, I enjoy looking at you. Your body. It makes me… What's the right word? Excited? No, that's not it. Horny? Yes, horny."

A spasm rippled through her inner muscles. "And you telling me what turns you on makes *me* horny."

Color crept up his neck to his cheeks. "I think I'll take that shower now. You can, um… If you want to, you can join me when you're done doing whatever you need to do."

His invitation too good to pass up, she calculated the speed at which she could swap out a two-handled faucet. "I want. Give me six minutes."

"Okay." He grabbed a towel from the linen shelves and hung it on the hook next to the tile-and-glass enclosure. "I need to…close the door first. I'll open it when I'm done."

"Perfect. That'll give me time to find my wrenches and plumber's tape." *And send a group text to the family.*

She retrieved her phone from her bag as the door clicked close. A few taps brought up a blinking cursor in the message bar of her family's group. "*Family meeting tomorrow night at 6:30. Attendance is mandatory.*"

If that didn't get the attention of her mother, father, sisters, and brothers, nothing would. The whole clan gathered for Sunday dinners, birthdays, and other special occasions, but calling a meeting was for serious business, like announcing her divorce from Derek. That had been the last time she'd gathered her family around her for moral support.

She switched off the ringer and stuffed her cell in her overnight bag. Her husband needed comfort and distraction more than her parents and siblings needed to ask questions she wasn't prepared to answer yet.

The bathroom door swung inward as she grabbed her bucket of tools. A shirtless Eli peered through the opening, but the shower drowned out whatever softly spoken words came from his moving lips. That mouth had kissed hers and urged her to forget the broken faucet.

He extended a trembling hand toward her and stepped into the doorway. His clothes were gone, but his erection hadn't waned in the least. "Can the plumbing wait until morning?"

Everything can wait.

Giving a nod, she set the bucket at the foot of the bed, stripped off her clothes, and freed her ponytail. His unwavering stare heated her skin faster than the air cooled it, assuring her the chemistry of their afternoon tryst wasn't a fluke. She closed the distance between them and caressed the light stubble on his chin. "Anything you want. I'm here for you."

CHAPTER ELEVEN

As much as he wanted to lift his wife onto the bathroom counter and lose himself inside her, Eli clasped Beatrix's hand and led her to the shower. She deserved better than a barbarian for a husband, no matter what the article he'd read had said about women liking alpha males. If he'd had the experience to have a style in the bedroom, it certainly wouldn't be bossy or aggressive.

She'd said not all women liked the same things during sex, but was it true?

The warm spray reminded him he hadn't showered before the mishap with the faucet. He hadn't gone to work, notified his students that he wouldn't be available during his office hours, or called the department chair to cancel their two o'clock meeting to talk about his research plans. At least he hadn't forgotten to show up for class today. He would, however, have to make arrangements for both of tomorrow's classes. How would he manage to do it all?

"Eli?"

The gentle brush of Beatrix's fingertips on his chest made him jump.

"Are you okay?" She cupped his jaw as she brought her body flush against his. "It's been a very emotional day for both of us, so it's okay if you're feeling anxious or overwhelmed."

He leaned into her touch, surprised at how much the anxiety faded away with her unexpected insight and understanding. "I'm just thinking about all the things I forgot to do today and the things I'm supposed to do tomorrow for work. I don't like giving anybody the chance to say I'm irresponsible."

"I'll be glad to set those people straight. Emergencies happen and you did what was most important in the grand scheme of things." A hug pressed her nipples into his skin, erasing his memory of all but the intense pleasure of their sexual encounter that afternoon. "We can fix everything else in the morning."

We. He had a partner now, in life, in parenting Eve, and in bed. *What if—*

"I know it isn't easy, but you really need to stop overthinking. It's our wedding night and, no matter the circumstances, we deserve each other's full attention." She locked her lips on his and guided him under the water.

Her kiss and the sudden sensation of floating in a calm ocean drew him away from the cares of the day, carrying him back to the moment when he needed a physical connection to her. He hadn't expected sex to be quite so mind-numbing or to have such a profound impact on his attraction to her. Maybe marriage would be better than he'd anticipated.

He slid his tongue along hers, grateful he'd been brave enough for a trial run of his online lesson in her truck. She moaned into his mouth as he led her in what the author of the article had described as a seductive dance. With his eyes closed, the sounds of the water and his wife's soft purrs mingled with the silky feel of her body pressed to his and the pressure building in his testicles. Then her fingers combed through his wet hair, massaging his scalp and relieving the rest of the tension in his body.

A groan escaped, but her responding hum and tighter grip on his head assured him he didn't have to hide his reactions from her. She'd told him she wanted to know what he was thinking and feeling—with or without words. Resisting the urge to smooth his palms along her wet skin and along the gentle curves of her hips wouldn't benefit either of them, not that he could control the desire. Her body fit against him perfectly when he cupped her bottom and pulled her closer.

She guided his hand to her thigh and hooked her leg around his waist. The position made his erection slip from her lower belly toward the place he longed to be. Only inches separated them from a sexual connection.

Her mouth withdrew from his and she panted against his neck. "I think we can skip foreplay. I'm ready, you're definitely ready, and the bed is too far away."

He gulped a lungful of air, caught between agreeing with her and wondering how sex in the shower worked without someone falling on the wet tile. "Here?"

"Here." She lowered her foot and guided him down onto the bench seat built into the back wall. "Sit."

As his naked backside met the smooth tile, she straddled his lap and lowered herself onto him in slow motion. Unlike their earlier sexual encounter, no layer of latex separated them. The slickness of her pulsing vagina generated pleasure a thousand times more intense than before. He gasped at the sudden squeeze and release of her body around him, captivated by the skin-to-skin bond she'd created. Every nerve jerked to attention and his testicles tightened, almost to the point of pain. His book knowledge about sex didn't approach the real act, and the riot of sensation zinging through every part of him transported him to a higher plane of existence.

She rocked forward and back, pulling him deeper inside her and into the surreal world of carnal pursuits. "Mmm. I hope this feels as good to you as it does to me."

"Better, maybe?" Wrapping his arm around her, he eliminated the space between them from the waist up. Her wet hair fell across his forearms and he threaded his fingers into the lush waves. "You can't feel this good."

"You don't think so?" She nuzzled his ear and arched her hips toward him again. "My G-spot begs to differ."

Embarrassment and a near miss with an orgasm brought a rush of heat to his face. Nothing he'd read had prepared him for the nuances of real intercourse.

She nibbled a path along his jaw and tilted his chin up before meeting his mouth for another breath-stealing kiss. Moving in time with the rhythm of each sweep of her tongue, she brought him to the edge again.

An involuntary buck triggered a release of pressure in his sac and a torrent up his length, but her throaty cry and rapturous expression as she dropped her head back launched him to paradise. No perfect test score or praise for being accepted into eight PhD programs matched the utter satisfaction of making love to this woman—his wife.

Chloe was right. I never should've doubted it.

He kissed Beatrix's bare shoulder and rested his head in the curve of her neck. Her jumpy pulse beat against his cheekbone, still as erratic as his own. No words formed in his brain, not even the poetic phrases that were easier to write than to speak. For once, his mind was clear.

Her fingertips spread across his spine and her belly tensed and relaxed against his ribs in quick succession. "Before you ask, that was amazing. Doing what married people do was an excellent suggestion."

"So you liked it, even though you did all the work?"

She leaned back, breaking their upper-body contact, and brushed away a tickly water droplet dribbling down his forehead. "Sex isn't work if you're doing right. It's even worth kneeling on hard tile. We should finish showering and go to bed."

"You should've told me it was hurting your knees." Planting his feet, he grasped her bottom and stood, much to the consternation of his rubbery legs.

She hooked her ankles at his lower back and hugged him like her life depended on him. "I'm fine. Put me down before you pull a muscle or something."

"You're not heavy." He carried her under the warm spray and battled the attack of nerves the thought of telling her the whole truth generated. Water splashed into his eyes, but he blinked and squinted against the mist instead of turning away. “And I like this…arrangement.”

Her lips curved into a smile that seemed genuine and possibly a little amused. “I like it too. However, it’s been a long day and we both need some rest, not that I’m opposed to more wedded bliss after we go to bed.”

“You’re very good at taking care of people.” He reluctantly raised her bottom high enough that his partially wilted erection slipped free, and then held on until she was steady on her feet in front of him. “I’m glad you’re here with me.”

“Me too.” She reached past him and picked up the soap. As she worked up a washcloth full of bubbles, a grin spread across her wet face. “You know, I was so disappointed last night when I left the coffee shop. I met a nice, smart man with similar interests and ruined it by jumping to conclusions. I’m lucky I got a second chance. Do you think PAID would pay us to endorse their services if we tell them we got married less than twenty-four hours after the mixer?”

“It would be nice to recoup the application fee, even though meeting you is worth much more than a month’s rent.” He lathered his hair with a squirt of tear-free baby shampoo. “A colleague recommended the service three weeks ago at lunch. She thought it would be easier for me to connect with someone if I met a limited number of prescreened women in a controlled environment.”

“She sounds smart. You need to thank your colleague.” Done washing, she pulled him back under the water and helped him rinse the lightly scented lather from his hair. The suds coursed down her arms and followed the contours of her body to pool at her feet. “*I* need to thank your colleague. And my sisters for butting into my personal life.”

“Do you have any regrets?” It probably wasn’t the wisest question to ask, but knowing where he stood might keep him from making more blunders.

Beatrix frowned. “About marrying you? Not yet. No. Just no. Do you?”

“No.” He sucked in a breath when she rubbed her still-sudsy washcloth down his chest and past his ribs. How could his body produce the beginnings of another erection already? "I, um…"

"You what?" Cupping his scrotum, she stared at him through her wet lashes.

"I think we should finish washing. And go to bed."

Her eyebrows rose, but her bland expression gave no hint about her mood. "I'm pretty sure that wasn't what you were going to say. You don't have regrets, but…"

Stilling her hand before she could grip his hardening penis, he fought to calm his racing pulse. "I didn't know what to expect. I don't have much experience. With women. Or sex. I know I have a lot of shortcomings, but I want to learn."

A quick smile drew his attention to her soft lips. "We'll learn together. Likes and dislikes. Everything. There's no pressure to get past a first or second date. We can focus on building a relationship based on honesty and trust. Personally, I don't think we have anything to worry about sexually as long as we respect each other."

Relieved by her understanding and logic, he nodded. "That sounds like a reasonable plan."

"Why don't you finish your shower while I dry off? I have a little surprise for you. A nice one. Nothing that'll make you uncomfortable." She opened the shower door enough to slip through and stepped onto the bathmat. "Did you notice my mom washed and put away all the towels we left on the floor?"

"Yeah." He swiped the sudsy washcloth under his arms and over the other mandatory washing places. "She even folded them the way I do. Should I send her a thank-you card?"

"You can thank her in person tomorrow evening. I called a family meeting at my parents' house to share our news." The pebbled glass between them blurred Beatrix's outline as she rubbed a blue towel across her back. "The sooner they know about you and Eve, the better."

"Okay. I'll try to make a good impression."

"You'll do fine. They're probably going to freak out a little at first, but don't take it personally. I went through a really rough patch and they worry about me sometimes." Her figure shifted toward the vanity. "Toothbrush. I knew I was forgetting something. Back in a sec."

Her casual insertion of mundane conversation soothed a jolt of anxiety at the thought of meeting her family. She would be there with him and, with luck, so would Eve. As long as he didn't let anxiety take control, he might not say or do anything stupid.

When he shut off the water a few minutes later, her unclothed silhouette hung the towel on the hook outside the shower and then disappeared into the bedroom. "I'll be waiting for you."

Not once in his entire life had he imagined himself in a situation like this—comfortable with a naked woman and grateful to have a partner, in and out of bed. She didn't seem to mind his lack of experience or his occasional inability to articulate his thoughts into intelligible words.

Chloe had rolled her eyes when he said marital love was for normal people. She'd insisted he was more normal than a lot of society, even if he wasn't average.

"Average is boring." Her gentle laughter echoed in his head.

Two weeks ago, she'd been alive and cheerful, despite her prognosis. She hadn't doubted for a moment he would meet someone who needed him as much as he needed her. She'd promised him happiness if he gave it a chance.

He combed his fingers through his towel-dried hair, regretting his procrastination in making an appointment for a trim. Unfortunately, finding a new barber had been low on his priority list. It still was. He had a wife and a baby to adjust to and the next few days would be a constant reminder that Chloe was gone.

"Hey, are you okay?" Although the hushed question came from behind, Beatrix faced him in the mirror, now wearing a nightgown that accentuated the soft contours of her body.

Beautiful.

She touched his cheek, wiping away a tear that had escaped without his notice. Then her arms circled his waist as she rested her head against his shoulder blade. Her silky hair clung to his still-damp skin and her body aligned with his. "It's hard losing someone you love.

I swear I won't tease you if you need to cry. I cried every day and night for months after my son died."

Amazed by her ability to read his mood every bit as well as his cousin, he covered her hands and linked their fingers together. The physical contact didn't chase away the burning sensation from the pooling tears, but it soothed the ache in his heart. "Did you have someone to support you? Besides your ex-husband, who didn't, I mean."

"My family. They've always been there when I needed them. " She tightened her hold on him and guided him to the bed. "They're your family now too, like Eve and me. We'll help you through this."

Unbidden and uncontrollable, streams of wetness rolled down his cheeks and dripped onto his chest. He sniffed against his suddenly runny nose. A simple acknowledgment stuck in his throat, so he joined her under the covers and buried his face in her chest to cry.

CHAPTER TWELVE

As Beatrix shifted Eve away from her breast, she surrendered to a jaw-stretching yawn and fought to stay awake. They'd left the hospital forty-five minutes ago, after a long day of drop-in feedings, funeral planning, and errands, but bedtime was still hours away.

Supper. Family meeting.

She adjusted her button-up shirt to cover herself before lifting the baby to her shoulder, gently patting her back, and setting the rocker in motion again.

"You have a full tummy, but I have no idea what Eli and I are going to eat." Even though a note from Chloe on the nursery dresser had said she wanted Elijah and his wife to be Mommy and Daddy to her daughter, Beatrix couldn't bring herself to use those names yet. The day after the poor woman's death was too soon.

Her husband knocked on the doorjamb and poked his head into the room. "I'm caught up with emails and phone calls, and I don't need to start the spaghetti for about an hour, so I was thinking about taking a nap. Is Eve asleep?"

Beatrix stood as she nodded, grateful for his initiative where supper was concerned. "Are you asking me if I want to join you? Because the answer is yes. I'm having a hard time keeping my eyes open."

"I'd like that." He crossed the room to her, his exhaustion clear but a relaxed smile forming when he touched a fingertip to Eve's full head of dark hair. "I can put her in the crib while you clean the tubing, if you want."

His willingness to risk another spit-up episode like he'd experienced at the hospital this morning caught her off guard. "Are you sure?"

"Yes." Curving his arms into a miniature cradle, he looked expectantly at her. "She can't splatter on me every time I hold her."

She grinned at his use of the vomit synonym he'd told her he had used as a child. Despite his unspoken doubts, Beatrix carefully placed Eve in his arms. "Probably not. I'll be in the bathroom if you need me."

The soft words he spoke to their newborn charge followed her into the hall, reinforcing her decision to stay positive about the impulsive actions that had brought her to this moment. They'd made love in a slow, healing way after crying together last night, and she'd awakened more optimistic than she'd dared in years. Strong incentive to succeed existed for both of them, in equal measure, unlike her failed marriage.

Why didn't I see it back then?

Now accustomed to the necessary job of cleaning the supplemental nursing equipment, she stood at the sink and strained to hear Eli's voice. Only a steady murmur carried from the nursery next door. His relaxed demeanor with Chloe's child spoke of an incomparable, immeasurable bond that had developed during the weeks he'd spent helping care for his cousin. He never stuttered or seemed to have trouble putting his thoughts and feelings into words with her. Eli and Eve would be as close as any biological father and daughter.

The barely audible pad of footsteps announced his presence at the bathroom doorway. "I told her a story about Chloe. Not a made-up story. A real one."

Beatrix turned on the hot water to rinse the tubing and held it under the stream. "I'm glad you can share happy memories with her. She'll really appreciate it when she gets older."

"That's what Chloe said. She made videos telling Eve about Brian.

How they met and how happy they were when they found out she was going to have a baby. That kind of stuff. It's important for her to know about them."

Touched by his sentimentality, she smiled at him as she hung the nursing aid to dry. "You're a special man, Elijah Clayton. No wonder Chloe chose you to raise her daughter. Let's go take that nap."

He reached for her hand and led her into their bedroom. His firm grasp suggested a need for someone to lean on, much the same as her. Without hesitation or noticeable embarrassment, he stripped off his clothes and climbed under the covers. Even as he adjusted the pillow, his eyes never seemed to leave her. "Your skin's pink from the tape again. Does it hurt?"

"Just a little. I washed off the adhesive and used the ointment the lactation consultant gave me. Hopefully, I won't need the tubing and tape anymore in a couple weeks." She kicked off her jeans and slid in beside him. His thoughtfulness encouraged her to snuggle close enough to tangle her legs with his. "Oh, we better set the alarm so we don't oversleep."

He laced his fingers through hers on his hip. "I set my phone for five o'clock. You can sleep longer if you want to since you had to get up to use the pump last night. I'll wake you when supper's ready."

"Thank you." She kissed his chin and closed her eyes.

If this was a dream, she hoped she never woke.

❧

GARLIC, OREGANO, AND BASIL SCENTED THE AIR, EASING BEATRIX from a restful sleep. She inhaled the delicious aroma again as she stretched, suddenly aware of Eli's absence and how hungry she was. When was the last time a man—besides her dad, one of her brothers, or a restaurant worker—had cooked supper for her?

Never. He ex-husband certainly hadn't made any effort to take care of her, except as an afterthought when he'd ordered takeout.

Her phone buzzed on the nightstand a second before she picked it up to check the time. Shelley's name and number flashed on the screen and then off again.

This ought to be good.

A few taps opened the text message.

"Who was the guy you were leaving the hospital with? Cute, by the way. And why were you carrying a baby? Does this have something to do with the family meeting???"

The cell vibrated in her hand and another message appeared.

"I promise I won't tell."

Ha. You can't keep a secret to save your life, Shell.

Beatrix tossed her phone toward the end of the bed and dug through the pile of clothes on the floor for her bra and underwear. The last thing she needed was her little sister hinting she knew what was going on and spilling her guts at the first push for more information from one of their siblings. Deciding how much to tell them would be hard enough as it was.

She stopped for a quick listen at the nursery door on her way to the kitchen, resisting a peek in the crib when no sound came from the room. Eve was real. This was her life now.

Halfway down the hall, Eli's voice broke the silence. "She taught me how to cook when I was in college. We spent a week making spaghetti, macaroni and cheese, omelets, and a bunch of other simple meals. The cake was lumpy and lopsided, but it tasted good. Oh, and she didn't make fun of me when I wouldn't touch raw meat and gagged at the sight of congealed soup from a can. They're really gross, so I usually eat vegetarian meals at home. I always wished she could've been my sister instead of my cousin. She was the best friend I've ever had."

From the swing several feet from him, Eve seemed entranced by his voice and methodical movements as he added pasta to a steaming pot on the stove. Her little legs danced in her footed pajamas when he glanced in her direction.

"Should we wake up Beatrix now? I mean Mommy. That's what we're supposed to call her." He laid the wooden spoon he'd used to stir the spaghetti across the top of the pot and walked to the swing. "You're supposed to call me Daddy, but I don't have any experience with babies."

The sexy combination of his bare feet, untucked undershirt, and butt-hugging khakis paired with the casual one-sided conversation with his rapt audience warmed Beatrix inside and out. She ambled into the kitchen and greeted her husband with a brief kiss. "You're a natural at it and Eve adores you. Thanks for letting me sleep."

"I should, um, check the spaghetti." He hurried to the stove and stirred the contents of the pot. "I don't know what kind of salad dressing you like, so I got out ranch and Italian."

"Either of those is fine." Instead of taking his sudden awkwardness to heart, she leaned down to smile at a wide-eyed Eve. "He's a good guy, isn't he? I should've trusted my gut reaction when we met. Can I help with anything, Eli?"

"No." His curt response might have bothered her if not for his wave toward the breakfast nook. Two place settings flanked a pair of salads on the modest-sized round table. A napkin-lined basket and the dressings filled the space in the middle. "Supper will be ready in eight and a half minutes."

"Okay. That'll give me time to check and change Eve's diaper." She reached for the strap holding the baby into the reclined seat.

"I changed it when I got up."

"I could've done that. You didn't have to do everything by yourself." If he tried to use it against her in an argument, she might have to smack him. Instead of removing Eve from the swing, Beatrix rubbed her finger across a tiny fist, still amazed and overwhelmed by the events of the past day and a half.

"You were supposed to sleep until we woke you. When supper's ready."

"I was hungry and I usually make my own supper." The justification sounded defensive to her own ears, but taking care of herself and everyone around her had been her self-appointed job for a long damn time. She plopped onto the floor in front of Eve, wondering how she would hide her uncertainties from her family—because they would notice if she hinted at any doubts about her relationship with Eli. "Maybe I should go by myself tonight."

Something clattered behind her, like he'd dropped something in the sink, making the baby and Beatrix jump at the noise. He mumbled something too low for her to decipher, but the clipped hiss of his unintelligible comment was almost certainly directed at her.

Without pulling her finger from Eve's firm grasp, she pivoted toward her obviously disgruntled husband. "Don't mutter under your breath. If you have something to complain about, at least have the decency to say it loud enough for me to hear."

His shoulders hunched and he stirred the pasta more briskly than before. The tension rolling off of him was almost as visible as the steam from the pot. "You're worried I'm going to embarrass you, aren't you?"

"*What?*" After carefully prying her finger free from Eve's fist, Beatrix pushed to her feet and crossed to the stove, forcing him to face her. "I didn't say or think that, so don't make assumptions."

"Then why don't you want me—us—to go with you?"

"I didn't say that, either." She shook her head and sighed. "I'm having a hard time separating being married to you from…my past experience. Derek, my ex-husband, did things with the expectation that I owed him because he did me a favor by helping. It wasn't obvious to me until you said you were making supper and that you'd changed Eve's diaper. I don't mind taking care of people, but he took advantage of it."

Eli narrowed his eyes and growled. "He was a jerk."

"Yes, he was. I guess, subconsciously, I'm worried you'll do the same. My family didn't object when I married Derek, but I don't think they ever really liked him."

Eli's lips flattened into a thin line. "You're worried they won't approve of me? Like my parents did to you?"

"No, not exactly." She raked her hands through her hair, finding a few tangles in the waves at the back of her head. "More like I'm worried they'll see that I'm unsure of my choices. I've never done anything close to this impulsive in my life and they're going to know I'm not as confident about my decision as I should be."

"If I'm not the reason you're worried, how will my being there make a difference? I thought we decided to support each other, no matter what." The frown softened. "Don't you trust Chloe's judgment?"

"I'm trying, but… Do you?"

"What choice do I have?" His simplistic assessment seemed as logical as her complicated one, and she didn't have an argument against his reason for going. They *had* agreed to be there for each other, and his cousin hadn't expressed a single misgiving.

"Okay, you're right. She wouldn't put Eve in a situation she didn't think was best for her. Maybe my hormones are going crazy from trying to induce lactation. And I don't want to fail. I'm sorry."

The frown deepened again. "My parents are the ones who should be sorry."

"Your parents are just being protective of you."

He snorted. "Overprotective, you mean. I'm used to having them question my decisions, but that doesn't mean they shouldn't apologize for being rude to you. Besides, I'm thirty-four, not sixteen."

"I'm going to give them the benefit of the doubt and assume finding out their niece was dying, her baby was born, and their son got married was too much all at once. If they still hate me a month from now, we have a problem." She brushed her fingertips along his lower lip, hoping to erase the worry. "Thanks for being patient with me. Having you with me tonight will feel like somebody's in my corner."

He kissed her finger and then her lips. "You were there for me, so I think it's *our* corner."

Does he even realize how sweet and romantic that is? Probably not. "I like sharing a corner with you."

Water sizzled and popped behind him, intruding on the intimate moment.

"Darn it!" He simultaneously adjusted the burner setting and swept the wooden spoon through the starchy bubbles overflowing the boiling pot. "Supper will be ready in three minutes."

❧

Beatrix sorted through the contents of the diaper bag a third time, certain she'd forgotten something important. *Diapers, wipes, change of clothes, bottle, formula.*

Did all new mothers worry about those kinds of things?

She hadn't in all the years she'd been babysitting her nieces and nephews, but Eve was *her* child, *her* responsibility. A last look around the nursery didn't reveal anything her parents wouldn't have at their house.

"Are you ready? It's five after six." Elijah stood in the doorway with the baby cradled in his arms, her precious face barely peeking out from the quilted pink blanket he'd wrapped around her.

On time and not afraid to behave like a good father. Her heart fluttered. *Oh my God, I'm going to fall in love with him.*

She cleared her throat and slung the diaper bag strap on her shoulder. "Ready. I just need to grab my jacket and purse."

Five minutes later, she slid behind the steering wheel of his car and focused on driving instead of her disconcerting realization. They didn't know each other well enough to develop an emotional attachment like love. It took time to see past the mirage most people showed the world.

Except he couldn't fake being nice and kind and thoughtful if he wanted to.

He was completely unpretentious.

"Are you nervous?" Eli's question came as she made the turn into her parents' neighborhood. "You're not usually this quiet. Not that you talk too much."

She nodded. "A little. Are you?"

His coat rustled against the passenger seat, suggesting a shrug. "Not as much as I thought I'd be. I'll have you and Eve with me."

"We're here." Streetlights flickered on when she followed the curve that led to the quiet cul-de-sac where the house she'd grown up in stood. The clock read eighteen minutes after six, and the driveway was empty of her siblings' vehicles. She pulled into the space in front of the garage door on the right and shut off the engine. "First ones to arrive.

That means we can tell my mom and dad before my brothers and sisters."

"Okay." Before she'd rounded the back end of the car, he had the rear passenger door open and the car seat unlatched from its base. "Eve's sleeping, so I didn't want to disturb her."

"Good idea." Carrying the diaper bag, she walked her new family to the front porch. The door swung wide as she reached for the doorbell.

Her parents glanced from her toward Eli and then the carrier hooked on his arm.

Deep breath and just say it. "Mom. Dad. I'd like you to meet Elijah Clayton, my husband, and our daughter, Eve."

CHAPTER THIRTEEN

"HUSBAND?"

"Daughter?"

The overlapping exclamations of Beatrix's mother and father broke the long silence, but as much as Eli wanted to retreat to the car, he didn't—because his leg muscles wouldn't cooperate and abandoning Beatrix seemed like a really bad idea.

Introductions. Act friendly. Be polite. Don't say anything stupid. "Nice to meet you, Mr. and Mrs. Glouster."

The woman aimed a familiar look at Beatrix, the your-explanation-better-be-a-good-one expression his mom had worn often during his childhood. A tight smile replaced it as she finally faced him. "Elijah. It's nice to meet you too. You'd better bring the baby inside. She's too little to be outside for long in this chilly weather."

Mr. Glouster stepped back from the doorway, his face a mask, hiding whatever he was thinking. "Elijah, good to meet you. Come on in."

Giving Beatrix's hand a gentle squeeze, Eli accepted his in-laws' invitation. Warmth seeped into his icy hand where it made contact with his wife's. Even with his somewhat lacking social skills, he would classify the welcome as unmistakably cool.

She walked beside him to the first room on the right—possibly a living room, although it was less formal than the one from his childhood. This one had a large basket of toys in the corner and four child-sized rocking chairs near a set of overflowing bookshelves.

Steady footsteps on the wood floor behind them signaled her parents had followed, but Beatrix didn't slow until they reached the adult-sized furniture. "I know this is out of the blue, but there were extenuating circumstances. Let's sit."

With a nod, her father sat in the chair and her mother perched on the arm. Beatrix led Eli to the couch adjacent to their shared seat. An end table separated them, and an intricately crocheted doily like the ones his great grandmother had displayed throughout her house rested beneath a squat candleholder.

While he unbuckled Eve and removed the outer layers keeping her warm, Beatrix summarized the major events of the past two days, including how they met. Thankfully, she left out the details of her departure from the coffee shop and what had happened at her condo when they'd gone to pick up her divorce decree.

Mrs. Glouster shared a look with her husband that reminded him of Chloe and Brian's way of communicating without saying a word. Then she pinned her gaze on Eli. "Eve is very lucky to have you. What you did for your cousin… It tells me you're a good man and you'll do everything you can to be a good father."

A compliment was a good sign, wasn't it? "I'll do my best."

"And you're happy with your decision to marry our daughter, even though you've only known each other since Sunday evening?"

He nodded, grateful for an easy question. "Yes."

She was silent as she stared at him, like she was trying to read his mind. "You understand marriage takes work, and adding a baby to being newlyweds makes it that much harder? The honeymoon is pretty much over."

"We didn't go on a honeymoon. Between finalizing the funeral arrangements, taking care of Eve, and my job, we don't have time. If we decide to take a trip after the semester's over, Eve will go with us. It depends on when Beatrix wants to go back to work."

The way she pressed her lips together in an upward curve hinted that he'd missed her meaning and responded literally to a figurative statement.

Looks like I ruined that first impression. That's nothing new.

Beatrix leaned close, her breath tickling his ear. "She's laughing at herself, not you. She made the assumption that you'd understand what she meant. Just tell her about yourself. It'll be okay."

Movement at his feet caught his attention, and he bent forward to lift a waking Eve from the car seat. She blinked up at him, grounding him and reminding him of his purpose as he positioned her wobbly neck in the crook of his arm. "Mr. and Mrs. Glouster, I—I'm on the autism spectrum. Asperger's. Sometimes, I misinterpret what people say and I can be socially awkward, but…I like Beatrix. She understands me better than most people and…and she loves Eve. Those are the things Chloe and I decided were most important when I signed up for the speed-dating event."

Rising from her spot on the arm of the chair, Mrs. Glouster smiled. "Thank you for telling us. I know it isn't easy to trust strangers with that kind of information. One of our grandsons is on the spectrum."

"Beatrix told me. That's how she knew I am, and she still married me."

"Yes, she did. Call me Maureen or Mom, whichever you prefer." Mrs. Glouster took two steps closer. "May I hold the baby?"

Fairly certain her words and actions indicated willing acceptance that he was her son-in-law, Eli stood and placed Eve in her arms. "Her name is Evelyn Briana. Evelyn is—was—Chloe's middle name and her husband's name was Brian."

"Perfect. Would you look at all that beautiful hair?" Maureen rubbed her cheek against the top of Eve's head, the same way Beatrix had done at least a dozen times today. "You're so precious. Oh, Paul, we have another granddaughter."

Mr. Glouster's unreadable expression became a grin as he extended his hand toward Eli. "Welcome to the family, Elijah. I think I can safely say we're happy to babysit if you and Trixie need a few hours to re—"

"Knock-knock! Trixie? Are you here yet?" A very pregnant woman who resembled Beatrix in hair, eyes, and facial structure waddled into the room with her coat flapping around her. She halted halfway to the coffee table, one hand at her lower back and the other on her protruding belly. It was larger than Chloe's had been right before Eve's birth. "Whose car is in the driveway? And what's the big an— That's him, isn't it? The guy from the hospital? And the baby. Well, I can tell this is going to be an interesting family meeting. Details. I want details."

Mr. Glouster guided her toward his chair as Maureen swayed toward the picture window overlooking what was probably the backyard. "Have a seat, Shell. We'll get started when everybody's here."

Shell let her coat slip down her arms into Paul's hands. "Maddie and Rob are helping Ty unload the computer and printer he got for you, Danny was just pulling in, and Em's right behind him."

As the woman sat, Beatrix slipped her hand into Eli's. Her voice was low when she spoke, probably quiet enough no one else could hear. "If this gets to be too much, let me know. Family meetings are usually loud and chaotic, and I've escorted Ian to the playroom more than once to escape the overstimulation."

Eli exhaled, grateful that she'd noticed the tension already building in his muscles from the steady hum of voices. "If it starts bothering me, I'll ask Ian if he wants to go too. Playing with Legos is therapeutic."

"Good plan. They're one of his favorite things to play with." Her smile triggered a burst of energy zinging through his insides. "We have a secret code, sort of like in baseball. Tug your right ear, brush you right hand along your right thigh, and make the Vulcan live-long-and-prosper hand signal above your knee. You've seen *Star Trek*, haven't you?"

He nodded. "Every episode. My favorite is when DS-9 revisits TOS and the tribbles."

"Mine too."

The background noise suddenly amplified, announcing the arrival of an equal number of adults and children and bringing the total to at least twenty people. They crowded into the living room as a single unit.

Murmuration, like a flock of birds.

Another slow inhale and exhale did little to calm the feeling of being buried alive. It even dwarfed the disconcerting sensation of walking into a classroom or lecture hall on the first day of the semester.

"Here he comes. I'll fill him in on the plan." Beatrix turned toward the group, wedging her thigh against his. Did she enjoy the contact as much as he did? "Hey, Ian! I want you to meet somebody."

"Hi, Aunt Bea." A lanky boy who reminded Eli of himself at the age of ten hugged her over the back of the couch. His crooked mouth suggested chewing on the inside of his cheek was a nervous habit, something else they had in common. "I finished the book about black holes last night."

She gave him a thumbs-up. "Cool. Did you like it?"

"Yeah."

"Good. I found another one at the library sale over the weekend. I'll bring it to Sunday dinner." Crooking her finger, she lowered her voice. "This is Eli. He's an Aspie too. I told him about our hand signal."

Ian's eyes flicked toward Eli and back toward Beatrix. "Really? Is…is he…is he your boyfriend?"

"Can you keep a secret?" At the boy's nod, she leaned closer. "We got married yesterday. You can call him Uncle Eli."

"You got married?" His exclamation brought instantaneous and absolute silence to the room, with the exception of a soft coo from Eve.

Eli tugged his ear for the third time, but Ian was clearly more interested in meeting his new cousin than escaping the din of nearly every adult still talking at once after his wife's announcement that, yes, she had gotten married and would be raising a baby with her new husband. Several of the eight children had gone to the kitchen with

Maureen to prepare a snack, but their voices carried down the hall to join the rest.

"You and my sister met at the speed-dating thing the other night, didn't you?" One of Beatrix's female siblings—the pregnant one, Shelley—cornered him next to the fireplace as she rubbed circles on her rounded belly. Her expression wasn't as welcoming as her brothers and sisters, their spouses, and their offspring. In fact, it was downright hostile, an easy read even for him. "I know darn well there's more to the story than Trixie let on. She never would've caved about going if she was already dating you. Okay, *maybe* she told Mom and Dad, but she didn't tell the rest of us."

His glance toward Beatrix was rewarded with the same sweet smile she'd greeted him with at table one, and it triggered the same she's-the-one feeling he'd experienced Sunday evening. How and when they'd met didn't matter.

"Don't bother to deny it." Shelley narrowed her eyes. "Who's Eve's mother? I swear to God if you have a wife or a girlfriend, I'll castrate you with my bare hands. My sister deserves better than another selfish jerk for a husband."

A pang near his heart popped the buoyancy Beatrix's smile had created. "My cousin Chloe. She died yesterday. From a brain tumor. Not long after Eve was born."

"Oh my God. Chloe Long? I knew she was dying, but I didn't know what was going to happen with her baby. Her husband was a firefighter." She froze midway through another small circular motion. "He died during a rescue earlier this year. I was working when they brought him into the ER. Eve's healthy, isn't she? No problems?"

He nodded, not sure he could speak past the lump in his throat.

"Thank God. I can't imagine what it would do to my sister if…" Her gaze skipped away and then back again. "You're the guy who's been visiting Chloe every day for the last two months. The whole hospital's been talking about how sad the situation was. I'm so sorry for your loss. And for thinking the worst. Geez, I had no idea." She gave him a sideways hug, but the state of her pregnancy still made the embrace awkward. "I'm Shelley. Please let me know if there's anything I can do. Babysit while you make funeral arrangements. Whatever you need."

"I did that today. Beatrix went with me."

"Of course. It's just like Trixie to step in and take care of everybody. I hope you know how lucky you are. She's the most selfless person on the planet." Shelley switched from rubbing her belly to massaging to her lower back.

"Do you need to sit down?"

"I'm fine." Her grimace suggested otherwise. "False labor again. It started a couple hours after I went to my checkup this morning. Do you know when calling hours and the funeral will be? I'll make sure the family knows."

He would've preferred to find an empty chair for her, but he was hardly an expert on pregnancy and childbirth. "Calling hours are tomorrow from six to nine and the funeral is Thursday at eleven."

"Okay. Does anyone have plans to serve lunch after the funeral? Brian's company from the fire station? Family? Church?"

Those things always seemed to happen, but he'd never given any thought to the logistics. "I don't think so."

"Then I'll talk to Mom about the arrangements for that. We can work out the venue and make sure there's plenty of food." After a few taps on the screen, she handed him her phone. "Here, put your number in my cell and I can text you once we have the details figured out. I'm guessing Trixie will be too busy with the baby to help. Diapers, feedings, laundry—on top of cooking and all the other regular stuff."

"I made breakfast and supper today, and I've been changing most of the diapers since she has to clean the tubing when Eve's done nursing. We haven't talked about laundry, but I don't expect her to do it by herself." He saved his contact information and held out the cell phone. A tiny wail almost made him drop it.

"Nursing? You mean she's trying to breastfeed? Like with a supplemental feeding system?"

"Geez, I should've known." Beatrix shook her head as she approached them and rocked the baby in her arms in time with her steps. "Shelley Marie, stop interrogating my husband. You always were too nosy for your own good. If I want you to know details about my personal life, I'll be the one to tell you."

"I'm just getting to know my new brother-in-law." Shelley's grin was cut short by a sudden gasp. "Yikes! I think my water just broke. The doctor said I was getting close but that I probably had a few more days to go before it was time."

"Deep breaths, Shell. Nurses aren't supposed to hyperventilate, especially when they need to call their doctor." Kissing her armful on the forehead, Beatrix turned toward him. "Eli, can you take Eve? She's getting a little fussy, probably because she wants you. I need to help my sister clean up so she's ready to go to the hospital when the doctor says it's time."

Glad for the reprieve, he focused his attention on Eve's scrunched up little face. It mirrored his current level of anxiety. "Let's go find the diaper bag and a quiet spot. I'll tell you about the clubhouse Chloe and I built when we were eight."

Shelley touched his arm as he turned toward the couch. "Look at her. She stopped crying as soon as you started talking."

Beatrix gave Eli another of her sweet smiles. "Because she recognizes his voice from before she was born." Then she pointed to the far end of the living room. "Try the third bedroom on the left. Light blue. Twin beds."

"Okay."

As he headed for the hallway, his wife took charge of the chaos. "Hey, Maddie, we need a bath towel. Ty, make sure you can get your car out. Rob, go grab the mop and tell Mom she's going to be a grandma again soon. Like tonight or tomorrow."

CHAPTER FOURTEEN

"BEATRIX?"

The mattress shifted, but Beatrix snuggled deeper into the covers, hoping whoever had whispered her name would go away so she could sleep a little longer.

"Beatrix, are you awake? You have a bunch of text messages from your mom."

Elijah. She sighed and struggled to open her eyes, still tired from last night's multiple feedings. Lack of sleep was one aspect of motherhood that would take getting used to. "You're home from work. What time is it?"

"One thirty."

"Already? You're late. Nobody gave you a hard time about taking this afternoon and tomorrow off, did they?"

"No. I got home over an hour ago. You and Eve were asleep, so I ate lunch and caught up on some grading before I came in to wake you." Eli's breath on her ear tickled all the way to her lower belly, but a tiny squall through the baby monitor nixed any thought of enjoying a bit of afternoon nookie. "It sounds like Eve's hungry again. I can make lunch for you while she's nursing."

Beatrix tilted her head toward him and she met his lips for an abbreviated kiss. "That's very thoughtful, but just a snack is fine. I had a light lunch before my nap. How about some cheese and fruit?"

"Okay." He placed her cell on the pillow as he sat up. "I'll change Eve's diaper and get the formula while you check your messages and tape on the tubing."

Before he moved out of reach, she placed her hand on his arm. "Thank you, Elijah. For everything. For the first time in my life, I feel like I have a true partner. It's…really nice."

The shy smile he gave her over his shoulder shone in his eyes and went straight to her heart. "I—" Another cry came from the monitor and he pushed to his feet. "She must be really hungry this time."

The flutter in Beatrix's tummy lasted long after his soothing voice silenced the baby's cries and she'd thumbed through the text messages from her mom. Shelley and Ty had finally welcomed their daughter into the world during her nap, but experiencing the giddiness of genuine affection for a kind and dependable man deserved an even bigger celebration. That expectation hadn't been on her radar when she'd reluctantly agreed to her sisters' prodding about jumping back into the dating pool after more than five years of being single.

Elijah's conversational tone carried from the nursery into the guest bath while she gathered the nursing supplies. Then his reflection appeared in the mirror, framing him and Eve in the doorway. He took a step closer. "Ready?"

Already falling head over heels for both of you. "Mm-hm. Shelley had her baby about an hour ago. Do you mind if we make a quick stop at the hospital before we go to the funeral home? You don't have to go in if you don't want to, not after everything with Chloe. I just need to give my sister a hug and tell her congratulations."

Relief slid over his suddenly tense features. "Okay. I'll wait in the car with Eve."

"Perfect." Beatrix gestured for him to lead the way to the nursery and followed him into the hall. "She's still so tiny, so avoiding hospital germs is a good idea. The visitation and funeral will expose her to enough bugs as it is."

"I don't want her to get sick."

"I don't, either." With the tubing in place, she sat back in the rocker. "Ready. We'll be protective new parents and not pass her around to everybody who wants to hold her. I found a sling on the bottom shelf of the changing table. People might be less inclined to ask about holding her if she's in that."

He placed the infant in Beatrix's arms and grimaced. "I tried it when Chloe and I were setting up the nursery, but it got twisted and tangled."

"I've used one before with my nieces and nephews. We'll figure it out."

"Okay. I'll go make your snack." His easy acceptance that she could fix the problem was clear in his relaxed gait out of the room.

Beatrix smoothed Eve's dark hair with her free hand as she cradled the baby against her breast and met the intent blue-eyed stare aimed at her. Innocence, intelligence, and an old soul resided in her eyes, surely seeing far more than simply the face of her surrogate mother. Beatrix would never be able to keep a secret—Santa Claus, the tooth fairy, and the Easter bunny maybe, but not her feelings—from this miracle child.

"I brought you a glass of water too." Eli's voice at the doorway drew Eve's gaze and her legs bicycled against Beatrix's arm. He crossed to the table beside the rocker, the glass in one hand and a plate in the other. "I read that breastfeeding mothers need to stay hydrated to maintain their milk supply. Since we don't know how soon you'll start producing milk, it's probably best to start now."

"Good idea. Thanks." She popped a grape in her mouth in an effort to distract herself from the slightly disheveled but sexy-smart man who no longer showed any sign of embarrassment at seeing any part of her naked body.

"You're welcome." After setting the plate on the table, he withdrew a coaster from his pocket and positioned the glass on it well away from the edge. "If you don't need anything else, I should call my aunt. She called while I was in class and I didn't see it until right before I woke you up."

"Why don't you invite her and your uncle over to see Eve? I bet they'd enjoy spending some time with their only grandchild. She's a bright spot in what has to be a terribly painful time for them."

The subtle tension in his jaw eased. "She asked about seeing Eve in her voicemail. I wasn't sure how you…if we… Technically, she has four sets of grandparents now. I'm not sure how to handle that."

Beatrix set the apple slice she'd picked up back on the plate and reached for his hand. His fingers threaded through hers as if it was the most natural thing in the world. "We're going to respect Mrs. Long's and Chloe's parents' right to get to know Eve, the same as your parents and mine. She's so loved and she deserves to grow up knowing that, especially when she's already lost the two most important people in her life."

"See? Chloe was right about you." He brought her hand to his lips and then kissed the baby's forehead. "She told me everything would work out the way it was supposed to, and it has. I better go call Aunt Elise."

If not for his transparent nature, Elijah's comments would've inspired an eye roll and sarcasm from Beatrix. His not-so-subtle told you so was probably about convincing himself, not her, even though his confident tone suggested otherwise.

As he disappeared into the hallway, she turned her attention back to Eve and lowered her voice. "Your mommy was right about *us*." The baby smiled around the tubing and nipple, making Beatrix fall even deeper in love with this perfect child. "And I'm a very lucky woman to have you and Eli in my life."

For the first time in six years, she wouldn't have to hide a shattered heart when she welcomed the newest baby into the family. Nor would she be the only one of her siblings without a child, something she'd been dreading since Shell and Ty had announced they were expecting.

Eli peeked around the doorway. "They'll be here in about a half an hour. And Aunt Elise asked about pictures. The ones from the hospital and some family pictures."

Eve's droopy eyes popped open, affirming Beatrix's speculation that the little girl recognized the man who would be her father in the coming years. "I should've thought of that. We'll take some while they're here and make time this evening or tomorrow for everybody else. Did the hospital say anything about newborn photos?"

"They're supposed to email me a link when the pictures are available. Chloe addressed the envelopes for the baby announcements before she had to go into the hospital. They're on the desk in the office. I just have to fill in the information on the card template and print them."

"I can help if you want me to." Beatrix shifted the baby to her shoulder and tugged her shirt over her breast. "You're way more responsible than you give yourself credit for. Chloe trusted you to raise her daughter and take care of the announcements and handle the final funeral details. You have nothing to prove, at least to me. You know that, right?"

He shrugged. "Sometimes I forget to do things. I'm better now that I make lists, but that's one of the reasons my mom and dad are so critical. They probably thought I forgot to tell them I was getting married, besides thinking I can't make an important decision without their advice."

"Maybe your aunt and uncle will put in a good word after their visit." She popped another grape in her mouth and then started the task of switching the tubing. "Do you know how long they're staying?"

"Aunt Elise didn't say, but I'll ask when they get here. They'll probably go home when my mom and dad leave." The tightness in his jaw eased as he crossed to the rocker, his gaze clearly on the baby. "I can hold Eve while you rearrange things."

"Thanks." She made quick work of the tape-and-tubing job while he cradled the wide-awake newborn. "Can I ask you a personal question?"

His grimace said he suspected it had to do with his parents. "I guess."

"When were you diagnosed with ASD? Or Asperger's, since it didn't used to be called ASD."

He placed the baby back in her arms and then shoved his hands in his pockets. "My first semester of college."

She waited through Eve latching on again for him to offer more details, but his mannerism gave away the anxiety her question had evidently sparked. Pointing it out would probably make him more self-conscious, so she reached for a cube of cheese. "How did you know to get tested?"

"One of my professors asked me about it. I was struggling with the group activities and went to her office to ask if I could do the projects on my own. She's on the spectrum too, so she recognized the issues I was having. I'm not sure she could do that anymore with all the self-identification rules. There weren't as many services available as there are now, but knowing what was wrong with me made a big difference in how I coped with the stress."

She cringed at his words. "I'm glad she helped you, but there's nothing *wrong* with you. Your brain just works differently. The tools for diagnosis are a lot better nowadays than they used to be. If you did well in school, your teachers and your mom and dad might not have noticed."

"They always knew I wasn't like everybody else, but they didn't know why. People thought I was weird. My dad wanted a son who was normal and my mom—"

"Elijah, you're thoughtful and kind, and that's more important than fitting society's definition of normal."

A hint of bittersweet smile showed itself when he met her gaze. "Chloe used to tell me average was boring."

"She's right. I'm glad you remember things about her that make you happy."

He dropped to his knees in front of her and wrapped her and Eve in a hug. "I miss her."

"I know." The words almost stuck in Beatrix's throat.

"WOULD YOU LIKE ME TO TAKE EVE FOR A LITTLE WHILE?"

Beatrix held her breath, hoping her husband had the courage to tell his mother the truth—that having the baby in his arms kept his focus from his dead cousin lying in the casket less than five feet away. Eve was the only reason the evening had been bearable for him.

After a glance toward Beatrix, he shook his head. Mrs. Clayton blinked at him as if she might demand an explanation, but he shook hands with a man wearing a shirt emblazoned with one of the local fire department's logo on the chest, oblivious to her expectation or purposely ignoring it.

The firefighter dropped his gaze toward the baby and blinked like he was holding back tears. "You look so much like your daddy. He was a good guy. Saved my life at least twice. I remember him telling the whole firehouse when he found out Chloe was pregnant. Man, he was so excited. It's not fair you that lost both of them. Eli, if you guys ever need anything, just stop by or call the station. I mean it. Anything."

Elijah nodded stiffly as the taller man swiped at his eyes and moved to the open end of the casket.

Beatrix slid her arm around his waist and leaned close enough to keep her comment private. "You're doing great. Let me know if you need a break. We can go for a walk. Or we can switch places so you can stand by Elise and Roger."

His tense shoulders dropped at least an inch. "I'm okay. I think. How much longer do we have to be here?"

The line still stretched along the wall and out the double doors across the room, but she pasted on a smile. "Only about an hour. Lots of people want to pay their respects. Looks like my mom and dad are here. There, in the doorway."

He glanced in their direction and then at her. "But they didn't even know Chloe."

"They're here to support you and Eve. You're as much a part of the family as I am. By extension, that includes Chloe."

"Oh."

His lack of insight into the kind of family dynamics Beatrix had grown up with made her itch to have a long chat with his parents. Unfortunately, jumping to conclusions and pointing out their shortcomings wouldn't help forge a good in-laws relationship. Why couldn't Roger and Elise have been his parents?

She kissed his cheek and then turned toward Eve's grandmother to check on the older woman. A flash of red caught her eye in the hall outside the viewing room, pulling her attention to a tall blond-haired man with an all-too-familiar swagger. Disgust almost forced a frown, but she gave Elise a sideways hug instead. "How're you holding up?"

Derek Marshall didn't deserve anything but a fleeting thought.

CHAPTER FIFTEEN

Elijah shook Mr. Glouster's hand and then took advantage of the opportunity for a calming breath when Mrs. Glouster gently hugged him around Eve. *Say the right words. Remember names. And introductions.* "Thanks for coming, Paul and Maureen. I'd like you to meet my parents. My dad, Eli Clayton, Sr. and my mom, Loretta."

The stark difference between Beatrix's parents and his mom and dad was all the more obvious in Paul's wide smile and his father's tight-lipped nod. Paul held out his hand. "Nice to meet you, Eli. Loretta. Elijah said you're visiting from Colorado. Beautiful state. Will you be staying long?"

Thank God! Now I don't have to ask.

The Claytons initiated more handshakes before Maureen spoke. "We'd love to have you over for dinner while you're here."

Elijah's mom glanced toward his dad. "That sounds lovely, doesn't it, Eli? Good to meet you both."

A long, uncomfortable silence dragged on for what seemed like an hour before his dad responded. "Paul. Maureen. We're planning to fly home on Sunday, so I'm sure we can make time to get to know our son's wife and her parents."

Okay. Sunday. I can last three and a half more days.

Maureen kissed Chloe's daughter on the forehead. "And Eve. She's such a sweet baby."

"Trixie? Is that you?"

Beatrix's mother frowned and turned toward the man approaching her from the left. "Derek Marshall. What's he doing here?"

Her tone was disapproving at best.

Derek. The jerk who blamed his wife for their son dying and then left her.

"Mom, let it go." Beatrix's fingertips barely grazed her mother's shoulder, but the light touch evidently was enough to stop Maureen from confronting the interloper.

Eve's sudden cry kept Elijah from handing her to Aunt Elise and punching the creep in the nose. One good hit would be worth the pounding the taller and bulkier man would likely dish out.

"Do you want me to take Eve?" Beatrix turned her back to her ex-husband and cupped the baby's head in her palm, but her eyes met Elijah's. "It's okay. He can't hurt me anymore."

"I left at least six messages on your answering machine in the last three days." Derek took another step closer, crowding into her personal space, something Eli had learned long ago could be as threatening as it was annoying. "Why didn't you call me back?"

She raised her chin, but she didn't move away from him. "I've been busy and we have nothing to talk about unless you need a plumber. Even then, I'm referring my customers to other contractors right now."

He grunted, reminding Eli of the enormous hogs he'd seen at the state fair as a young boy. "That isn't what I wanted to talk about. Whose kid? And how do you know Chloe Long? I'm her life insurance agent. Was."

A serene smile spread across Beatrix's face, causing a hiccup in Elijah's pulse. "The baby is Chloe's daughter. I—my husband and I—are her legal guardians. I'm her mother. Elijah, this is Derek Marshall. Derek, this is my husband, Dr. Elijah Clayton. Chloe's cousin."

Derek's jaw dropped. "You got married? When did that happen? I didn't know you were even dating anybody."

"We're divorced, Derek. My personal life is none of your business." She glanced over her shoulder and lowered her voice. "Oh my God. The phone calls. You didn't actually think I'd take you back after the way you treated me, did you?"

The angry flush across his cheeks almost matched his red tie.

"I guess that answers my question." Her hair swayed back and forth as she turned away from him again. "Just so we're clear, I have no interest in reconciling, reconnecting, or whatever it is you think you want from me. Please pay your respects to Chloe and leave. You've already caused a scene. Don't make it worse."

Her expression held none of the bitterness or regret Elijah expected, only annoyance—the same kind she'd aimed at him when he'd asked the wrong questions at the coffee shop. He would never forget that look as long as he lived. Hopefully, she wouldn't need to aim it at him ever again.

"Are you okay?" Beatrix's soft words soothed the twinge his memory caused as Derek made his way past the head of the casket without even slowing and then headed for the exit.

"Yes." He was better than he'd been in weeks—because she cared if he was okay.

"Good. There are just a few more people in line and then we can go home. Eve will be hungry soon." She turned toward his parents and sighed. "I'm so sorry you had to see that."

His mom patted her arm. "No need to apologize for your ex-husband's bad behavior. You were considerably more polite than he deserved."

"Still, this isn't the time or place for—"

"Really, Beatrix, it's all right. His behavior is his own to apologize for, not that he seems inclined to do so. You didn't let him draw Elijah into his issues with you, and you stayed between him and Eve."

His dad grimaced, the mannerism everybody seemed to notice they shared. "*We* should be apologizing to *you*. I let concerns about my son's welfare influence my feelings about you. It wasn't fair to either of you. I'm sorry."

"I am too." Gathering Beatrix into her arms, his mom gave her a gentle hug, the kind Elijah had treasured as a child. "He and Eve are lucky to have you."

A quick blush spread across Beatrix's cheeks, making her even prettier than before. "Thank you. I think we're pretty lucky to have each other."

I must not have screwed up too badly then.

The final group moved from Mrs. Long toward the casket, shaking hands and offering their condolences to his parents, Beatrix and him, and then Aunt Elise and Uncle Roger. The end of the line also left incredible relief in its wake as the last visitors finally joined several others near the doorway.

I want to go h—

A robust cry brought his attention to Eve. Her tiny scrunched face matched his mood—tired, hungry, and beyond ready to leave.

Beatrix rubbed her palm along his bicep and kissed his jaw. "You look as cranky as she sounds. Come on. I'll order a pizza and we can pick it up on the way home."

"Okay." He leaned into her caress, savoring its calming effect. "I'll eat anything but sausage and hamburger. Gross texture."

"That makes it easy. I can hit reorder on the app and we're good to go." Grasping him by the elbow, she turned toward their families and Mrs. Long as she yawned. "We hate to rush off, but it's time for Eve's feeding and tomorrow's going to be another long day. Goodnight, everybody. See you in the morning."

A chorus of farewells erupted and he added his own before she led him across the room and to the exit. They paused at the coatrack long enough to put on their jackets and bundle a fussing Eve in her blanket. Brisk air crept in around his neck when they stepped outside, but he'd take the cold over a drawn-out departure any day.

She aimed the key fob at the car and the lights flashed on and off to signal the doors had unlocked. "If you put Eve into the car seat, I'll start the car so it can warm up."

"Okay." The baby's cries became full-fledged squalling as he fastened the latch, locking her into the seat. She paused for a full two seconds when the engine started, but then picked up where she left off. "Should I ride back here with Eve? I don't like it when she cries."

"Sure. It's normal, but I don't, either. Check the inside pocket of the diaper bag. I think I saw a pacifier in there. It might make her happy until we get home. Are you buckled?"

He double-checked the strap across his lap and shoulder as he unzipped the bag, the steady noise of Eve's crying pushing him to hurry. "Yeah. What does a pacifier look like? Is it this pointy thing with a squishy ball on the end?"

Beatrix's laughter joined Eve's wailing, making him wish he had a bottle of pain relievers and a quiet room to himself. "Um, no. Sorry. Sorry for laughing. That's a nasal syringe. You know, for removing the goopy stuff from her nose."

"Ew. That's disgusting." He fought his gag reflex through more amusement at his expense and continued his search of the pocket.

"Well, she doesn't exactly know how to blow her nose. Look for a soft plastic thing with a ring-shaped handle on one side and a nipple on the other. A bottle nipple, not a breast nipple. There's sort of a disc-like shield in the center. The nipple part goes in her mouth so she can suck on it."

Headlights flashed through the car, illuminating the new item in his hand. "I think I found it."

"Good. Hold it to her lips to see if she'll take it. If she moves toward it, guide it into her mouth. But don't force it."

"What if she doesn't want it?"

"Then we listen to her cry the rest of the way home. At least fifteen minutes by the time we stop at the pizza place. Or you can let her suck on your finger, which isn't a good idea unless you washed your hands very recently. Too many people germs from shaking hands tonight."

Desperate to quiet the gasping cries, he carefully touched the protruding tip to Eve's bottom lip. Silence fell as the pacifier disappeared into her greedy mouth. "Finally. Is this going to last until we're home?"

"Maybe? Eventually, she's going to realize nothing's filling her tummy. Just make sure it doesn't fall on the floor. That might mean catching a slobber-covered pacifier in your hand."

The glow of passing streetlights lit up Eve's undulating cheeks and wide eyes. Her gaze seemed fixed on his, like she doubted he had the fortitude to touch her saliva-drenched bribe.

Do I?

"Did you hear me, Eli? Do *not* let that pacifier get dirty, or we're going to have hear the starving-baby symphony the rest of the way home."

"Okay." He could tolerate a few germs better than the heartrending cry of a hungry baby. *Probably.* "Are we almost there?"

"Four blocks from the pizza shop. I'm a regular, so they should have the order ready when we get there." At the next stoplight, Beatrix looked over her shoulder and smiled. "Parenting is hard, and you're doing a great job, especially considering you don't have any previous experience with babies."

Her compliment made breathing easier and soothed some of the anxiety trying to push him into panic mode. "You're a lot better at it than I am. I always worry I'll do the wrong thing."

Green light formed a halo around her head as she faced the windshield again. The hum of the engine changed when she accelerated through the intersection. "I've had years of practice and all parents make mistakes. The fact that you worry means you're probably doing okay. Besides, Eve doesn't care if you're perfect. Don't tell my brothers and sisters, but neither am I."

A streetlight lit up her face in the rearview mirror, revealing a slight grin that suggested she enjoyed the dynamic he'd witnessed with her siblings. They knew they could depend on her, but they'd also supported her decision to marry him and become Eve's mother. Shelley hadn't questioned her sister's choice, only his motives.

They were protective of her, not entirely unlike the way his parents had always tried to protect him.

He adjusted the blanket that had slipped away from the car seat and confirmed that Eve was still in possession of the pacifier. He would protect her, try to keep her safe and happy. "Nobody is. I sort of understand why my mom and dad worry about me so much now. Protective or overprotective, I'm glad they apologized to you, though."

"Me too, for your sake. When we stopped at the hospital to visit Shell and the baby earlier, she said she was sorry for interrogating you. I told her she had to tell you, not me." The car slowed as she made a left turn. Neon signs glowed in the windows of the short row of shops, casting red shadows over the car's interior. Then the whooshing of the heater fell silent. "We're here. I'll be back in a jiffy."

The car locks snicked closed as she stepped up onto the sidewalk, matching the imaginary click of everything in his life fitting into place. Maybe he wasn't as self-confident as Beatrix, but the outright rejection of her imposing ex-husband had boosted Elijah's ego and impressed his parents. She'd chosen him and claimed she was lucky to have him.

The only times he had ever been a first choice were related to academics—school and work. Thankfully, he'd sort of fit in with the brainiac types and their quirky behaviors.

Her black dress shifted around her calves when she entered the shop, bringing his attention to the legs she wrapped around him while they had sex.

Making love.

She preferred to call it that. The term hadn't seemed accurate at first, but the more time he spent with her, the more comfortable the words became. Either way, what they did together in bed—and the shower—was so much more than the physical relationship he'd expected to be ambivalent about. It brought sexual and emotional pleasure.

Chloe had been closer to him than any other person in his life, but Beatrix held an intimate connection to him, one he'd never experienced before.

Is it because I'm in love with her?

He dug his phone out of his pocket and typed the question he had no answer to in Google's search bar.

"What is romantic love?"

The massive list of results popped up on the screen as she reappeared on the sidewalk with a pizza box.

CHAPTER SIXTEEN

"I APPRECIATE YOUR UNDERSTANDING, MRS. Z, AND MACK PROMISED me he'll be there by ten this morning to fix the leak. Talk to you soon." Beatrix ended the call and shoved the cell phone into her robe pocket, grateful Eve had been fascinated enough by the spinning mobile above her crib not to demand an immediate diaper change and feeding. "Sheets. Did I remember to put them in the dryer last night?"

"I did." With half his face hidden behind a stack of folded laundry, Elijah hurried into the nursery. "They're on top. The rest goes in our bedroom. Have you seen my shoes?"

"I think I saw one sticking out from under the couch last night. Or was that the night before?" She grabbed the pile of rainbow-hearts bedding and set it on the dresser. The nearly endless goings-on of the last five days had run together, but she wouldn't give up the wonderful chaos for a billion dollars. This new life was so much better than the lonely existence she'd chosen after the loss of her son and the divorce. She was the closest she'd been to a whole person in a long time. "Did you pack a piece of pie in your lunch? I know my family is just trying to be helpful, but they need to stop with the four-course dinners already."

"I forgot about lunch. I'll go do that now." He adjusted his hold on the armload as he turned toward the hall, but he stopped inside the doorway. His backward glance hinted he had something on his mind.

A full minute of fidgeting and lip chewing passed before she closed the distance between them. "What's bothering you?"

"Nothing. I—I…" He shook his head and looked toward the floor.

"Hey, it's okay. Talk to me. Please?"

After a long moment, he finally looked her in the eye. "You shouldn't have to remind me to do things like packing my lunch."

She cupped his clean-shaven jaw in her free hand and kissed his cheek. "We all forget stuff sometimes. The laundry would still be in the washer if you hadn't finished it. No keeping score, okay? We're here to help each other, especially while we're getting used to parenting a newborn, being married, and learning how to balance everything. A lot has happened in the last week."

The tension seemed to dissipate from his shoulders and he let out a breathy sigh. "I couldn't do this without you."

"That makes two of us. I—"

He jumped when a vigorous cry came from the crib. "She gets louder every day. I hope it doesn't mean we're bad parents."

Beatrix tried to hold in a chuckle and failed. "I've heard a lot worse from my nieces and nephews. She's learned that crying gets our attention and we give her what she needs. It's completely normal. Now go, before you're late for class. And if you forget your lunch, I can bring it when I pick you up at quarter after ten for Eve's appointment with the pediatrician."

"That's a reminder, isn't it?" Before she could answer, he touched his lips to hers, inciting a pleasant quiver in her tummy. "Thank you. I promise to be ready and waiting for you."

You're the sweetest man I've ever met.

Another squall made her wince, and she gave her husband a gentle push toward the hallway. "You need to go. I'll see you in a few hours."

He nodded and headed in the direction of their bedroom, the stack of laundry still piled in his arms. Less than a minute later, as she lowered Eve to the changing table, he hurried past again. "Shoes. Lunch. Computer bag."

A smile etched dimples into Eve's plump cheeks and she turned her head in the direction of Elijah's voice. Her attention clearly focused on his repeated words carrying to the nursery, Beatrix made quick work of the wet diaper.

"Lunch. Computer bag. Ten fifteen." The clunk of a door closing announced his departure and the faint hum of the garage door opening followed. Steady knocking began almost immediately and a muffled yell followed. "Forgot my keys!"

"Your daddy is adorable." Still getting used to referring to Eli as Eve's father, Beatrix eased the baby's legs back into her pajamas. Practice seemed like the only way to get used to respecting Chloe's wishes.

Eve lifted a tiny fist to her chin and then scrunched her face into a pout. Her mouth had evidently been the target. As Beatrix snapped the sleeper closed, another bout of fussiness segued into a full-blown demand for food, drowning out the continued knocking from the direction of the kitchen.

"Almost ready. We have to help Daddy first." She scooped the baby into her arms and hurried to the kitchen. Spying his keys in plain sight on the counter, she detoured to pick them up on her way to the door.

The look of horror on Eli's face as she opened the door to the garage spoke volumes about his level of anxiety. "Is Eve sick? Maybe you should call the doctor's office to see if you can take her sooner. Should I stay home?"

Eve finally took a breath at the sound of his voice, giving Beatrix a moment of silence to kiss her husband on the lips and press the key ring into his outstretched hand. "She's just hungry. She'll be fine once her tummy's full. Here are your keys. See you after your morning class."

"You're sure?"

She swayed back and forth, in hopes of having, but hardly expecting, an effect on the baby's crying. "Positive."

Although his creased brow suggested he didn't believe her, he grabbed the doorknob and pulled. "Okay."

"I love you." The door banged closed before she caught—and

finished saying—the spontaneous words that had snuck out. "So, I didn't see that coming."

Why did most major life events happen to her without any warning?

Eve took another gulping breath, releasing Beatrix from the stunned realization that Elijah had quietly snuggled his way into her heart since their six-minute conversation just over a week ago. "I'm so sorry, sweetie. Let's go take care of your breakfast while I mull over what to do about your father."

She retraced her steps to the nursery and crossed to the rocker. A few adjustments to her robe and the tubing prepared her for what had become an easy, if not always convenient, habit. "Maybe by next week we won't need this anymore. I know I won't miss all the extra work, and I'm sure you'll appreciate not having to wait."

Eve immediately quieted and latched on without any encouragement. Wide blue eyes locked on hers as Eve nursed, the wisdom in their depths nudging Beatrix to talk through the sudden feelings that seemed as natural as loving her parents, her siblings, and the child in her arms.

"What should I do? We've only known each other a week and I don't want add to his stress and anxiety." Beatrix leaned against the padded cushion lining the back of the rocker, trying to force her body to relax, even if her mind refused. "It isn't supposed to happen this fast."

Eve's cheeks and jaw paused their enthusiastic motion as she blinked.

"You think it's that simple, do you?"

The baby resumed her suckling with another slow blink.

"Okay, maybe you're right. Love isn't supposed to make sense. Look at Aunt Shell and Uncle Ty. Who would've thought a light-saber-loving systems analyst could fall for a high school science teacher in a Spock costume at a Halloween party? At least she didn't make me dress as an Ewok for their wedding. Of course, Ty threatened her with Ferengi ushers and Klingon vows. I'm pretty sure the truce will end the first time they take Autumn tricking-or-treating. Thank God she's too young to dress up this year."

A trickle of formula leaked from the corner of Eve's lips when she smiled.

"Yeah, they'll probably do it anyway, just to show her off to everybody who stops by their house. What do you want to be for Halloween? A puppy? A kitty? Or maybe a cute little baby dragon? And we can take pictures to give to all your grandmas and grandpas." She lifted a tiny fist to her lips and kissed her daughter's delicate fingers. "How did I ever get so lucky to be your mother, my sweet angel?"

Her phone vibrated against her hip, but twelve minutes couldn't have passed during the one-sided conversation. She slipped her cell from the robe pocket and tapped in her passcode to access the text message that appeared on the screen.

"Did Eve stop crying?"

His concern warmed Beatrix's heart. *"Yes. Happy as a clam now that she's eating. You're a good father to worry about her."*

"I'm more worried I'll do something wrong and she'll hate me."

By the time she read the message, another popped up.

"You're a good mother."

"Thank you :) I stand by what I said. You're a good father, and Eve could never hate you after all you've done for her and Chloe." The urge to say she loved him was strong, but a text wasn't the right time or place to make that kind of pronouncement. *"See you after class."*

":)"

Warmth changed to contentedness, a feeling she hadn't experienced in a romantic relationship until now. "Your mother was a smart woman, Eve. I wish we could've gotten to know her."

"Hi, Eli. Do you have plans for lunch?"

Elijah deleted the last of the junk mail from his inbox before checking the time and looking up at Dr. Bell, the colleague who occupied the office next to his. "Twelve thirty already? Hi, Izzy. I brought mine today, but I can go with you to the food court to eat."

"Thanks." She smiled, probably because she was grateful she wouldn't have to eat alone. His faculty mentor had almost as many insecurities and anxiety issues as he did. "Are you ready now, or do you need to finish what you're doing first?"

"I think I'm ready." Checking that his keys were in his pocket, he stood and picked up his lunchbox from the desk.

She led the way out of the building and to the adjacent one, thankfully as comfortable with the lack of conversation as he was. At the entrance to the student center, she veered to the left and he continued through the occupied tables to their usual spot in the corner.

As he emptied the contents of his lunchbox on the table, a young woman from his Intro to Creative Writing class waved from the booth against the near wall. *Yvette Harris.* "Hey, Dr. Clayton, your speed-dating haiku this morning was awesome! So much more inventive than the boring stuff my high school English teacher made me read. I can't wait for Wednesday's class."

Heat crept up his neck beneath his collar, but he gave her a closed-mouth smile and a nod—the standard reaction he'd adopted when he didn't know how to respond to a student outside of class. At least she hadn't asked a question or moved to his table.

Izzy set down her tray across from him and dragged her chair closer as she sat. "Speed-dating haiku? Is that good or bad?"

"Both." He unwrapped his peanut butter sandwich and took a bite.

"I guess I missed a lot while I was at the symposium in Cincinnati. Dr. Windsor told me your cousin died while I was gone too." After removing the safety seal and lid from her yogurt parfait, she looked up at him. "I know you were expecting it, but it must've been horrible. Are you okay? Oh, and what about the baby? Are you still going to raise her?"

Backtracking through Izzy's inquisition, he washed down a bite of peanut butter and bread with a drink of vanilla rooibos from his insulated bottle. "I'm mostly okay, and Eve too. One of the women at the speed-dating event had to leave to deliver a baby as soon as I sat down at table ten. But I met Beatrix at table one and we went for tea. I liked her, but she thought I was a pervert and left when I started asking about breastfeeding. Then the bathroom faucet broke and she came to fix it. While she was there, Chloe called to say it was time, and Beatrix went with me. And Eve was born and we got married and Chloe—"

"You got married? To a woman you met at the speed-dating event?" Izzy's eyes widened. "The same day?"

"No, the next day. The faucet broke while I was getting ready for work in the morning. Beatrix is a plumber. And a songwriter and musician."

"That's so…impulsive. And romantic, in a scary sort of way. I don't think I could marry somebody I barely know." With a spoonful of blueberries and yogurt halfway to her mouth, she leaned forward and lowered her voice. "How did you know she's the one? Did it just…*hit* you? Like you *knew*?"

"Chloe said she was. I trusted her judgment, and she was right. Everything kind of landed in place before we had time to really think about it. I think I might be in love with Beatrix. I have all the symptoms, and sex is nothing like I expected." Judging from Izzy's bright pink cheeks and sudden interest in digging for a piece of granola, he probably shouldn't have mentioned that last bit. "Sorry. TMI."

She cleared her throat and finally looked up at him. "It's okay. Have you told her?"

"That I'm on the spectrum? Yeah. Actually, she figured it out and asked me." The crust peeled off the bread in a long strip as he slowly rotated his sandwich.

"I mean that you love her. But that's good. I think telling somebody you're autistic is harder. I'd rather be rejected because the other person doesn't feel the same than have them judge me for something I can't control."

"No, I haven't told her. I'm not sure she'd believe me if I did. Her ex-husband was—is—a jerk." The urge to punch Derek Marshall in the nose still lingered. "He came to calling hours and was rude to her."

"That's crappy. Do you show her? By helping with laundry and dishes and taking care of the baby? Actions are more important than words. People use words to lie and say hurtful things." Izzy dropped her spoon in the parfait and frowned. "Evan proved that last year."

Not surprised by the direction of their conversation, he made a note in his phone to thank the department chair for assigning him a mentor who could relate to him and vice versa. "I make supper and she loads the dishwasher most of the time, and we both do laundry. If it's feeding time and I'm home, I change Eve's diaper while Beatrix gets the formula pouch and tubing ready. I want her to know I'm responsible enough to handle being a parent and a husband."

"What did she say about you being on the spectrum? When I told the man I went out with after Evan, you'd think I said I had Ebola or something equally deadly and contagious." Her deep frown and scrunched forehead made her feelings about that incident obvious, although her words did an excellent job of conveying them too. "I'd rather have ASD than be an ignorant ass. At least I know what's wrong with me."

"ASD is definitely better than Ebola and being a jerk. Beatrix says it doesn't bother her. Her nephew is on the spectrum." The sandwich lost its flavor with the realization that his mentor probably didn't have any more insight than he did into how to show his wife he was falling in love with her—and that left only one option. "I think I might have to tell her, like when she's doing something nice for me. Maybe ironing my pants when I forgot to hang them up and I'm running late for work."

Pausing with the spoon still stuck in her mouth, Izzy sat back in her chair. After a truly gross audible swallow, she pulled the utensil free. "I did that once, and the next day he told me he was being transferred out of state for his job. I saw him a couple months later in the grocery store, so I'm pretty sure he lied. At least you're already married. It's harder to dump someone when you have to get a divorce."

"A *divorce*?" The few bites of sandwich in his stomach clumped into a knot. "I can't tell her if she might divorce me."

Izzy tore open her package of pretzels with cheese dip and dunked a stick. "Probably best to show her and hope she doesn't get mad."

CHAPTER SEVENTEEN

Basking in the afterglow of slow lovemaking, Beatrix finally admitted to herself what she'd suspected for at least two days. Eli was more than a husband of convenience and her feelings for him had changed into a much stronger emotion than simple affection. His willingness to leave behind his comfort zone and share equal parenting responsibilities made up only a small part of the evolution.

Good father. Good husband. Good friend.

The best lover.

She kissed his neck and thanked whatever lucky star had seen fit to guide this man into her life. "I love you."

Taking her with him, he rolled toward his side of the bed until she lay on top of him. His fingers strolled along her spine like they always did after their nightly session of sexual exploration. His silence didn't surprise her, given his frequent unawareness of unwritten communication practices. He'd gotten better at it in the bedroom and when his work schedule required an adjustment, but an "I love you" was a big thing in their small world. He deserved a little patience after all that had happened to disrupt his life since July.

A move. New job. Chloe and the baby. The search for a partner and marriage. When he was comfortable and sure of his feelings, he would share them.

She closed her eyes to savor his gentle touch and the scent of his warm skin. Their breathing slowed to a lazy rhythm, drawing her toward sleep.

"I didn't expect marriage to be like this." His softly spoken words caressed her soul the way his fingers caressed her skin.

"It isn't like this for everybody."

He drew light circles on her lower back, barely skimming the upper curve of her bottom. "I remember when I used to visit Chloe and Brian before I moved back to Colorado. They were always happy. At least I thought so. They held hands and kissed a lot. Not like one of the other faculty in my department. Her husband came to pick her up two weeks ago since her car was in the shop. He started yelling at her about spending money on new tires as soon as she opened the door and then he drove away without her. On Friday, she told me they're getting divorced."

"Good for her. Her husband sounds like a jerk. About a third of us make the choice to get divorced or have it made for us."

His hand stilled. "Do you regret it?"

"Regret that things didn't work out with my first marriage?" Surprised at the simplicity of the answer, she shook her head. "No. I'll always mourn the loss of my son, but I don't regret Derek's choice to leave. I deserved better. Besides, I wouldn't have you and Eve if things had been different. I'll never be sorry for that."

"I'm not sorry, either." The subtle curve of his lips against her cheek sent a long pulse of pure happiness to her heart.

Together, their breathing slowed, lulling her toward sleep and dreams that could never inspire wishes for more than she'd been blessed with on the day she'd married this man.

"Your lunch!" Beatrix grabbed the insulated bag from the kitchen counter as the door into the garage closed.

The lock clicked and the door swung back open, framing her harried husband. Dark circles shadowed his eyes from too little sleep, courtesy of a newborn who wanted her daddy to hold her all night long. "Is today Friday yet?"

She offered a weak smile and handed him the forgotten lunch. "Only Wednesday. Did you remember your phone and your wallet?"

He patted his pockets and then nodded. "I think I have a meeting at four, so I'll be later than usual getting home. How about spaghetti for supper tonight? Or I can pick up pizza."

"Don't worry about it. I'll put something in the Crockpot before I head over to Maddie's to start on the bathroom remodel." Leaning through the doorway, she cupped his cheek and touched her lips to his. "Maybe the noise will keep Eve awake most of the day and she'll sleep tonight. Drive safely. I love you."

"Okay. I'll start laundry when I get home and load the dishwasher after supper. Gotta go." The tension in his jaw eased and he kissed her once more before he hurried to his car.

She waved as he backed out of the garage, determined not to take his lack of verbal response to her words personally. His experiences weren't the same as hers, not with family, friendships, or romantic relationships. Besides, they'd met a week and a half ago—a short time to fall in love by anyone's measure.

Hoping for a quick shower before Eve woke for her breakfast, Beatrix hustled to the master bath. A few missed clippings from Eli's morning shave littered the counter, but he'd put away his electric shaver and rinsed the toothpaste from the sink. Exhausted or not, she was a lucky woman.

Cooler-than-usual water chilled her skin, but it chased away the sleepiness and forced her to hurry through washing and rinsing. As she dried, faint cooing carried from the baby monitor on the dresser, warning her the call for mealtime could come at any moment.

Ten days. Life had changed so much in a week and a half. *And I wouldn't trade it for anything.*

She pulled on a pair of jeans and one of her work shirts before heading to the kitchen for formula and to the nursery to suit up. Bright eyes stared up at her when she finally peeked over the crib rail. Then tiny feet kicked at the blanket that no longer covered the baby to her chest, and Eve stuffed a little fist in her mouth.

"Well, it looks like *somebody* got enough sleep last night." Beatrix picked up her daughter and kissed her adorably plump cheek. "Good morning. Are you ready to learn about plumbing today?"

The fist escaped and a squall followed, showing off Eve's developing personality.

"Okay, food first and then plumbing." Settling in the rocker, Beatrix positioned the demanding angel at her breast. "I get cranky when I'm hungry too, but we need to work on your manners. Grams taught me you're supposed to ask politely. Can you say please?"

Eve paused in her vigorous sucking and blinked up at Beatrix, like she might be considering the request.

Thrilled not to be on the receiving end of another must-have-Daddy hissy fit, Beatrix brushed her fingertips over the baby's feathery tufts of dark hair. "Close enough for now."

Nine o'clock arrived by the time they finished the feeding, started supper in the slow cooker, and managed a bath and dressing in clothes that didn't double as pajamas. Her phone buzzed against her backside as she stuffed enough supplies to last the day into the diaper bag.

"I'm coming, Maddie! Boots. Where are my work boots?" She dropped a kiss on Eve's head as she passed the swing on her way to the bedroom. "Almost ready to go, kiddo. I'll never complain about anybody with kids being late ever again."

When she pulled in her older sister's driveway twenty minutes later, Maddie bounded down the front porch steps and jogged to the truck. Her smile widened as she stopped at the driver's door.

Returning the grin, Beatrix lowered the window and tossed the diaper bag to her sister. "Here, make yourself useful. You know, you could have another kid if you love babies that much."

Laughter chased away Beatrix's frazzled brain as Maddie caught the overstuffed tote. "Hey, Trixie. Hallie's already more than I can handle some days. I swear that girl's six going on forty with a side of menopause this week. I just want to get my baby fix and send them back home with their parents."

"What are you going to do when she's a teenager?" Beatrix shooed her sister out of the way and opened the door.

"Buy stock in hormone pharmaceuticals? She'll be PMS-ing and I'll be approaching perimenopause. Rafe may have to build himself a man cave in the basement." Maddie slung the strap over her shoulder as she peeked in the extended-cab window. "Do you want me to carry Eve into the house so you can get your tools?"

"Sure, but don't let me keep you if you need to get stuff done. I thought you were working from home the rest of the week." At the rear of the truck, Beatrix slid her bucket of tools and the duffle of work towels onto the tailgate.

"I am. She can be my assistant." The top half of her sister disappeared into the backseat. "Well, look at you, all wide-awake and smiling this morning. Are you ready to crunch numbers with Aunt Maddie? And we can take selfies and send them to Grams."

"That doesn't sound like work to me."

"All work and no play is for the birds. Besides, I had to meet with a new client Saturday morning. I deserve a half day off." With the car seat handle hooked over her arm, Maddie shut the truck door. "Ready?"

"Yep." Hefting both items, Beatrix followed her sister into the house. "Part of your babysitting job today is making sure Daddy's girl is awake as much as possible. She's been keeping Eli up for hours at a time the last three nights, just wanting to be held—and only by him unless it's feeding time. The poor guy was dragging this morning."

Maddie set the car seat on the kitchen table and tugged off Eve's hat by the tassel, making every strand of coal-black hair stand on end. "You sound like your cousin Hallie. She had her days and nights mixed up for the longest time. How about if we unbundle you while your mommy starts the demolition? I bet that's her favorite part of the job."

"Third favorite." Heading for the guest bathroom, Beatrix tossed a grin over her shoulder. "Getting paid is the best part of every job, and finishing so I get paid is a close second. I'd tell you to give me a holler when Eve's hungry, but she's getting pretty good at doing that herself."

"This little angel? No way. Mommy's exaggerating, isn't she? You're too sweet to holler." Her sister's baby talk and soft cooing followed her down the hall.

Unlike her most recent plumbing job, she drained the pipes before attempting to disconnect the water lines for the sink, toilet, and shower. Getting drenched had been a small price to pay for all she'd gained in the week and a half since that mishap, not that she hadn't deserved a wake-up call after her misjudgment of Elijah on their post speed-dating date. Her gut instincts had never steered her wrong, and she would've ended up in the same place if she'd listened to them when she met him. How had her life changed so much in so little time?

Tiny squalls came from the direction of Maddie's office as Beatrix carted the sixty-year-old baby-blue toilet tank toward the garage, signaling a mandatory break. "Hey, Mad, I'll be there in a few minutes! Take Eve to the window so she can look outside. It might distract her until I prep a batch of formula and tape on the tubing."

A careful twist of the knob and a nudge with her foot eased the door open while she clutched the awkward load in her arms. She'd learned an important lesson very early in her career—never, ever drop a toilet on a ceramic tile or concrete floor.

After several slow steps into the garage, she squatted to lower her load onto the layers of cardboard she'd laid out earlier. Halfway there, a twinge in her chest muscles almost loosened her tenuous grip on the tank. Another cramp hit as she released her hold and straightened. Matching dark spots spread in two large lopsided circles on her shirt, chilling her skin.

"Looks like I should've packed extra clothes for me too." She stalked to her sister's home office and joined Maddie at the window overlooking the backyard. "Got a shirt I can borrow? You, Em, or Shell could've warned me about leaky nipples."

CHAPTER EIGHTEEN

Rolling toward Beatrix's side of the bed, Eli stretched, only to find an empty expanse of cold sheets instead of his wife. He frowned as he squinted at the glowing numbers on the clock.

6:00 a.m.

No red light shone on the baby monitor setting beside the clock. Had she gotten up early or had she not come to bed last night?

She hadn't awakened him, but a tornado siren probably couldn't have roused him after a twelve-hour workday yesterday and three nights spent soothing Eve. He'd barely had the energy to kiss his wife, eat a late supper, and hold his daughter for a few minutes before surrendering to the need for sleep.

He shoved aside the blankets and reached for his robe as he climbed out of bed. Low singing drew him to the nursery when he exited the bedroom.

Beatrix sat in the rocker with the baby cradled in her arms. She looked up at him and smiled, triggering the familiar tickle in his stomach. "Did you sleep well?"

"Maybe? I don't remember." Something about her seemed different, but he couldn't quite place the change. "Did you come to bed last night?"

She shook her head, and her hair fell from her shoulder to her bare breast, where their daughter nursed. "I put Eve in the swing and slept on the couch, sort of, so you could get some rest."

"The tape. That's what's missing." Eve reached her tiny hand toward him, and he extended his finger for her to grasp. "Did we run out of formula already? We just bought a whole case a few days ago."

"We still have plenty. My milk came in while I was working at Maddie's yesterday. I'll have to feed Eve more often until I'm producing enough, but that means you can feed her with a bottle sometimes now if you want to. And we don't have to mess with the tubing anymore." She yawned, reminding him he'd finally gotten a decent night's rest and could use another.

"It should make night-time feedings faster." He kissed Eve on the forehead as he eased his finger free from her loosening grip. Then he touched his lips to his wife's, wishing he had time to make love to her before he left for work. "Thank you for letting me sleep."

She tugged on his robe, pulling him close enough for another kiss that made him wish for a lazy Saturday morning. "You're welcome. You'd better go take a shower and get dressed. The calendar says you have to be in your office at eight o'clock for a meeting and I promised Maddie I'd be at her house by eight thirty."

With a nod, he reluctantly straightened and headed for the bathroom. At the bedroom doorway, his feet slowed of their own accord —maybe because of the feelings inundating every muscle in his body, including his heart. *I love you.* "I, um. I'll see you in the kitchen."

Without glancing his direction, she took a drink from the water bottle in her hand. "Okay."

He trudged into the hall, fighting a frown. As much as he wanted to say the words, they wouldn't come out. Another conversation with his mentor seemed to be in order.

❧

FAIRLY CERTAIN IZZY HAD FORGOTTEN ABOUT MEETING FOR LUNCH, ELI tapped the dark screen on his cell to check the time again. A text popped up a second after he entered his passcode.

"Oops. Sorry. Got distracted by the paper I'm submitting today. Lunch tomorrow instead?"

Considering he'd committed the same faux pas a month ago, he could hardly blame her. That he needed advice today of all days was beside the point. "*Tomorrow's fine.*"

"Clayton, right? Elijah. English Department. We met at the new faculty orientation in August. Dash. Morley Dash. History. The Renaissance, to be precise." The chair across from him screeched against the floor and a vaguely familiar man set his tray on the table. "Do you mind if I join you?"

Saying yes would be rude, wouldn't it? Eli tore a piece of crust from his sandwich, not that his stomach was in the mood to eat. "No."

Dr. Dash dropped into the seat and peeled away a section of paper from his wrap. "You got married recently, didn't you? Congratulations. Oh, and the baby. A girl, I believe? My condolences for the loss of your cousin. I overheard the department's administrative coordinator talking to Dr. Bell last week about the situation."

Nodding, Eli didn't even attempt to keep up with Morley's chatter. His brain didn't have the energy for people today.

"I must say I'm impressed by how quickly you met your wife and got married. I've been searching for true love for over a year with no luck, even after all the research I've done on how to woo women and the many ways to please them. I'm easily the most romantic man I've ever known." Dash bit into his sandwich, offering a short break in the one-sided conversation.

"Maybe…um, maybe you can…help me then." Eli set aside his sandwich and picked up one of the triple-chocolate cookies his sister-in-law had sent home with Beatrix yesterday. "I, um… I don't know how to tell my wife I love her. I've been doing the dishes and laundry and helping with Eve, but I want to do something romantic. She slept in the living room with the baby last night to let me sleep. And I don't know how to show her that I appreciate it."

Morley's smile widened as he leaned closer, but it didn't seem like a teasing grin. "You've come to the right person, Elijah. I know all about what women want. Do you see to her needs? Sexually, I mean. Men can be selfish about satisfaction in bed without meaning to. It's all about that drive to propagate the species. You know, biology. You'd think evolution would've taken into account the risks of overpopulation. It seems to me a reduction in testosterone levels in men would be a more efficient means to control population than the increase in diseases—infectious and otherwise—in addition to ensuring the mothers of our species experience equal pleasure. You do give her as much pleasure as you receive, don't you?"

Heat crept up Eli's back, spreading to his neck and ears. He stuffed a bite into his mouth to keep from over-sharing and nodded.

"Have you considered telling her? Just saying the words?"

Eli washed down the bite of crust with a gulp of apple juice. "Actions speak louder than words. Besides, my mouth refuses to cooperate every time I try to say it. My cousin said Beatrix was the one for me. I still don't know how she knew, only that she was right and I'm sad that she isn't here to see it or help me tell my wife how I feel."

"What you need is a plan." Morley sat back in his chair and drummed his fingertips on the table. "A romantic dinner with her favorite meal, champagne, candlelight. Definitely a nice tablecloth. Some soft music. A gift. Yes, a necklace, or perhaps an engagement ring if your whirlwind courtship and marriage didn't allow for it, culminating with a marriage proposal on bended knee, of course. Then the *pièce de résistance*—the suggestion that you renew your vows at the soonest convenient time. If that doesn't convey how you feel about her, nothing will."

"I don't drink alcohol." Despite the confidence his lunch companion exuded, Eli aimed a frown at the self-proclaimed expert. "How do you know it'll work if you've actually never tried it?"

"Research. Ten years of it, covering two thousand years of historical anecdotes and hundreds of romance novels. The progression of modern romance novels alone speaks to how important honesty and enthusiasm are in marital relationships, especially to women." Morley sighed. "If only I could find the right woman myself. You're a very lucky man. You must make every effort to show your wife how much you treasure her. Ooh, you write poetry, don't you? You need to create a masterpiece about your feelings for her."

"The last original poem I recited in front of her made her cry. The bad kind."

"Then this is your opportunity to erase that memory and forge a new one with positive feelings. One that bares your very heart and soul." Morley swapped his wrap for the coffee he clearly didn't need, given the speed and profuseness of his remarks. "Let's outline your plan."

Abandoning his sandwich, Eli opened a new note on his phone. "Okay. You seem to know what you're talking about. Dinner. Candles. I don't know if we own a tablecloth."

"Then you'll have to pick one up while you're shopping for dinner and the gift." Dr. Dash recited the list again as Eli tapped in each entry. "And I recommend implementing our grand plan on Friday or Saturday evening so that you may enjoy each other's company without having to rise early the next morning."

"Tomorrow is Friday." Eli closed his eyes and breathed to calm his suddenly thudding pulse.

"No need to panic, my good fellow. I'll donate the tablecloth, candles, and sparkling cider." As Eli opened his eyes, Morley slid the cell phone across the table and added to the list. "Order dinner online and pick it up on your way home tomorrow. Did you give your bride an engagement ring?"

"We didn't have time to get engaged."

"Then you'll need to decide what kind of ring suits her." Looking up from the screen, his advisor took another drink from his coffee cup. "Tell me about her. What would you say is most important to her?"

Glad for an easy question, Elijah picked up his sandwich again. "She's a plumber, musician, and songwriter, and family is most important to her. She's an excellent mother and has a nice smile."

Morley nodded and made another note. "She'll appreciate a simple but elegant solitaire, perhaps in the baby's birthstone. I believe tourmaline is the gemstone for October. It comes in a variety of colors. Your jobs are to buy the ring, write the poem, and order dinner. I'll drop by your office in the morning with the rest of the necessary supplies. Yikes! I need to run. Class in twenty minutes."

Before Eli caught up with the rapid-fire instructions, his lunch companion gathered his meal and dashed toward the closest exit. At least Morley had left his phone on the table instead of necessitating an exhausting chase and second conversation of the day.

He hurried through eating, staving off a bout of low blood sugar taking precedence over his lack of hunger. The decision proved wise when his four-thirty appointment with a student turned into a long discussion about the difference between compare and contrast.

His phone buzzed against his leg as he finally walked to his car at seven forty-five. Multiple text messages appeared on the screen, the last setting off instant remorse for losing himself in grading.

"Please answer!!! Where are you???"

He almost muttered a self-deprecating insult, but a small group of people stood a few feet away from his parking spot. Talking to himself tended to earn him weird looks. In the driver's seat, he tapped in the only response he could. *"I'm sorry. I just saw your texts. I was grading and didn't realize what time it was. I'm in the car and ready to come home. Are you mad at me?"*

"We'll talk about it when you get home. Drive carefully."

She was mad all right, of that he had no doubt. His parents had used those exact words on numerous occasions during his high school and undergrad days, and it had never ended well.

Every possible consequence invaded his thoughts on the drive home, but he focused on the road and the other cars. An accident would only give her more reason to be angry and destroy his romantic plans for tomorrow.

The entrance into the kitchen opened as the garage door rose, and Beatrix stood framed in the doorway when he shut off the engine. Her arms were crossed in front of her chest, and the sweet smile she'd given him at the PAID event hid behind a frown like the one that had greeted him during the plumbing disaster.

With his computer bag hanging from his shoulder and his lunch box in his hand, he climbed out of the car to face her wrath. Each step that carried him closer to her made his stomach cramp, but she didn't move or speak.

She followed him into the kitchen and closed the door. "I was worried about you. All I could think was that Eve and I had lost you, that something awful had happened again."

Guilt threatening to steal his voice, he set his belongings at his feet to shed his coat. "I'm sorry. I'll try to do better."

Her arms closed around him from behind and she hugged him. "I wasn't mad, just concerned. You've gotten very good about communicating with me, except this one time, and I know you're trying."

He shifted so he faced his kind and forgiving wife. His belly rumbled, but her mouth tempted him more. A soft kiss led to another and another, until her lips parted and she welcomed him inside. Each slow glide of her tongue along his eased the tension in his neck and shoulders. Making love ranked higher than food or sleep at the moment.

A faint cry preceded a seconder louder one—and a groan from Beatrix. She rested her forehead against his chest and sighed. "Eve must have heard you. I'll heat up some supper for you while you go get her. It's almost time for her nurse again anyway."

He barely refrained from voicing his own groan. "Okay."

The cries grew louder as he hurried to the nursery and ended as quickly as they'd started when he lifted Eve from the crib. He kissed her pink cheek and laid her on the changing table, as their routine had been since she'd come home from the hospital.

She blinked up at him and smiled.

"You look like Chloe when you smile. Sometimes, it almost feels like she's here with me. Do you think she's watching over us? I wonder if she can see how much you've grown. Do you remember her? She held you when you were born. I have pictures. Maybe some day they won't make me sad." After a few adjustments to her clean diaper and a squirt of hand sanitizer, he eased her tiny legs back into the footed pajamas and refastened the snaps. Somehow, they all lined up correctly on the first try. "I think I'm getting better at dressing you, don't you?"

The scent of food lured him back to the kitchen and the woman he loved. He would tell her tomorrow—through words and actions.

Beatrix set a bowl on the table next to two slices of buttered bread. "The last of the vegetable soup my mom brought over last weekend and homemade bread from Maddie. You look tired. How about if Eve and I sleep in the living room again so you can finish catching up on your rest?"

CHAPTER NINETEEN

Fighting a yawn, Beatrix popped the screw onto the Phillips-head bit. It dropped to the floor as she raised the drill toward the hardware for the new toilet paper holder and bounced behind the commode for the third time in less than five minutes. "Dang it. You don't want to go in the hole? Fine. I give up, you little twerp."

"Hey, Trix, I have to say I'm impressed by your lack of expletives." Maddie stood in the bathroom doorway with a wide-awake Eve cradled in her left arm. "I think I can handle putting in the last screw. The bathroom looks great, by the way."

Beatrix's attempt at an eye roll only succeeded in making her bleary eyes water. "I know for a fact you've never used a drill. Do you even own a screwdriver?"

"I don't know. Rafe probably has one in the garage." Her sister aimed a goofy grin toward Eve, earning her a smile. "Your mommy is so silly. Come relax and have something to drink, sis. You've been working your hiney off all day. Milk, juice, water, or tea?"

"Water's fine." Beatrix retrieved the runaway screw and set it inside the roll of plumber's tape on the new granite counter to try one more time before she headed home. "What time is it?"

"Almost four thirty."

"It feels like midnight. I may sleep all day tomorrow." Too tired to think about gathering her tools, Beatrix followed Maddie down the hall.

"Go get comfortable and I'll grab your water. Somebody has sucky face again." Her sister paused at the family room. "Hallie, move your toys out of the recliner please. Aunt Bea needs a comfy place to sit while she feeds Eve."

"Okay, Mommy." Clad in an oversized black shirt that hung halfway down her shins and a crocheted doily clipped to the collar, Maddie's daughter picked up a serrated butter knife, several crayon drawings, and a pair of shorts with what seemed to be a paint stain. A double row of stuffed animals lined the couch on the other side of the room.

Beatrix bit her lip to keep from snickering. "Who's on trial this time, Judge Hallie?"

"Whiskers the kitten." The girl frowned. "The prosecution has nothing but circumstantial evidence, and the motive is weak. I think the jury is going to acquit."

A snort snuck get out, but Beatrix covered it with a cough. "What's the crime?"

"Someone stole the last piece of birthday cake." Hallie leaned a little closer and tossed a glower at the stuffed audience behind her. "I'm supposed to remain impartial, but I think the thief was Josie Giraffe. She's the only one tall enough to reach the kitchen counter."

"Ah, but kitties can jump and climb." Beatrix dropped into the chair and raised the footrest. "What makes you so sure Josie did it?"

"No paw prints. There was a smear of frosting on the cake plate, and the lick marks were too big for a cat. Remember when we went to the zoo and saw the giraffes using their tongues to reach the leaves outside their fence?"

Her shirt and bra unfastened, Beatrix pulled the receiving blanket from the back of the chair and draped it over her left shoulder and breast. She yawned as she sank deeper into the recliner. "Maybe you should be a detective instead of a judge when you grow up."

Hallie shook her head, making the loose bun at her neck wobble.

"Detectives can't be on the Supreme Court. Besides, I want to be the boss of Daddy. He's only an attorney."

A bark of laughter finally escaped. "Only, huh?"

Eve in one arm, a glass in her free hand, and humor dancing in her eyes, Maddie entered the family room. "Judges have to remove their courtroom attire before they make cookies. Go wash your hands and get out the ingredients for no-bakes. It's junk food night in the judge's chamber. And Daddy's bringing home pizza for supper, so you better not let him hear you saying he has an inferior occupation."

"Yay! Cookies and pizza!" Hallie yanked her makeshift robe over head and tossed it on the jury before racing past her mom.

Lowering the baby into Beatrix's arms, Maddie grinned. "Looks like my six-year-old is acting her age again. I'll keep her busy so you two can have some peace and quiet. Oh, and I changed Eve's diaper right before we came to see you."

"You have no idea how much I appreciate that at the moment." After settling Eve at her breast, Beatrix took a long drink from the glass her sister handed her. "Not that I'd trade anything in the world for this parenting gig."

"I'm so happy for you, Trixie. I can't imagine how difficult it's been to watch the rest of us have kids after what happened." Maddie gave Beatrix a sideways hug. "Elijah and Eve are so lucky the speed-dating thing worked out. He's obviously crazy about you."

A smile came harder than it would have a few days ago since he still hadn't told her he loved her, in spite of the fact that she'd shared her feelings for him often and it didn't seem to bother him.

A thud made them all jump, and Maddie rushed toward the kitchen. "Yell if you need anything. Hallie, are you okay?"

Faint giggles assured Beatrix her niece had survived whatever mishap had occurred during her ingredient-gathering mission, and she folded the blanket to frame Eve's face. "When you get bigger, we can make cookies together too. I bet Daddy would help. He likes to cook, and he adores you."

Eve stared at her like she understood every word.

"I hope he comes home on time tonight. We've hardly seen him the last few days." Beatrix swallowed past the lump forming in her throat, hoping against hope his absence wasn't a sign that he'd tired of her attempts to get a response—any response—from him.

Cheerful voices carried from the kitchen, a deeper one now among them, meaning Rafe had arrived home earlier than usual. Listening to her sister's happy little planned family only added to the wavering confidence Beatrix had in her own unconventional and unplanned marriage-and-family situation.

Tears tried to leak down her cheeks, but she swiped them away. She wasn't a crybaby or a drama queen. Life wasn't always fair, and she'd accepted it as the only absolute when her divorce had been finalized. Being a mother meant making sacrifices, and falling in love was no guarantee of happily-ever-after.

Determined not to let the green-eyed monster gain control again, she focused on Eve and the newfound freedom to nurse her child on her own. Life was better than it had been for a long time.

As Beatrix fastened the last button on her shirt, Maddie poked her head around the doorway. "Supper's on us tonight. I had Rafe bring home an extra pizza and breadsticks as a thank you for doing the bathroom project, especially when you're still adjusting to all the changes. We could've waited another month or two, but you're taking care of everybody like you always do."

"Middle-child syndrome. I'll invoice you in a day or two." Beatrix lifted the baby to her shoulder and nuzzled the soft tufts of dark hair. "I'd planned on picking up something on the way home, so thanks. Do I get cookies too?"

"Hallie boxed up a dozen for you and put them in the fridge. She left a note on top of the pizza box so we don't forget to grab them when you're ready to go. Do you want me to take Eve while you pack your tools?"

"Still haven't satisfied your baby craving, huh?"

Her sister shrugged as she crossed to the chair. "She's such a sweetheart, and I'm definitely not having another kid. Let me have my fun."

Passing off her daughter, Beatrix laughed. "You're going to have to get a puppy."

"Keep your voice down. Hallie and Rafe have been conspiring to convince me we need a dog." Maddie kissed Eve's cheek and sighed. "You're every bit as cute as a puppy, and you don't shed."

"She's also going to take a lot longer to house train." Beatrix pushed to her feet and stretched. "This chair is entirely too comfortable. I should have everything loaded and ready to go in fifteen minutes. Can you pack the diaper bag for me?"

"Already done." With Eve cuddled against her chest, Maddie retreated toward the kitchen. "We'll snuggle until it's time to put her coat on."

A yawn forced Beatrix into motion. Falling asleep wasn't an option, not if she wanted to finally spend some time with her husband —if he came home at a decent hour.

Thirty minutes later, she shut off the engine and closed the garage door behind her truck. Eli's car sat in the other spot, sparking hope she might stay awake long enough to make love with him tonight.

She slung the diaper bag on her shoulder, cradled Eve in her left arm, and balanced the three-box-high stack of supper in her right hand on the way to the door into the house. It swung open as she approached. "You're home early."

"I have important things to do here." Eli scooped up their daughter and greeted them both with a kiss. Then his slight smile slipped into a grimace. "You brought pizza."

"Rafe and Maddie wanted to thank me for the bathroom job. And I, for one, am too tired to cook." She waited for him step aside so she could put the rest of her load on the table.

He didn't. "But… But…"

"But what?" Although his lack of words grated on her exhaustion, she took a deep breath and called on every bit of her patience. "What's going on? Just talk to me."

The aroma of something familiar mingled with the garlic-and-oregano scent from the pizza and breadsticks. Then her cell buzzed against her hip.

He chewed on his lip and shifted his weight from one foot to the other.

Her mouth watered after another sniff. "Is that my mom's barbecued ribs? Pizza can go in the fridge for lunch tomorrow if it is."

The tension seemed to drain out of his body, and he finally walked into the kitchen. "I asked your mom what your favorite meal is and she made it for us."

"That's so incredibly sweet and brave. Thank you." She set the boxes on the counter to make space in the refrigerator. "Eve nursed right before we left Maddie's and she shouldn't need a diaper change for an hour or two."

"Okay."

His footsteps faded as she stacked several containers to clear a shelf and slid the boxes into the fridge. After a quick peek at the contents in the oven, she retrieved plates and silverware. The least she could do was set the table after he'd made such thoughtful supper plans.

As she placed the last fork next to her plate, he padded back into the kitchen, sporting that nerdy-sexy look of an Oxford shirt and khakis, bare feet, and Eve in his arms. Mussed hair and a few days of beard stubble added to it.

Swoon.

He stopped near the baby swing and frowned. "I already set the table."

"What?" She straightened the fork, fairly certain he would if she didn't. "Like in the dining room? We never eat in there."

His gaze darted from her toward the floor and then in the direction of the dining room. "I…I thought we could tonight."

"But ribs are messy and you'll want to wash your hands. Don't you think it'll be easier to eat in the kitchen?"

Indecision seemed to weigh on his mind for a long minute before his shoulders slumped. "Okay."

Too tired and hungry to deal with sulking, she bit her tongue and walked to the fridge. "I'll pour drinks while you put Eve in her swing."

He didn't respond, but the creak and click behind her confirmed he'd followed her instructions. Then a chair scraped across the floor as she hefted the milk. A heavy sigh carried to her ears.

She whirled around and plunked the gallon jug on the table. "Elijah, will you please just tell me what's bugging you? I'm tired, I'm hungry, and I don't feel like playing guessing games."

His jaw tightened and his lips almost disappeared behind the grim line of his mouth. Everything in his demeanor said he had no intention of sharing his thoughts.

A surge of guilt tried to attack her conscience, but she refused to pussyfoot around his feelings while hers fell victim again. "Whatever. Let's just eat so I can go to bed."

His utter silence during the meal she should've thoroughly enjoyed but barely tasted confirmed her suspicion. He'd shut down—not that she had any clue why—and nothing she said or did would make a difference.

As soon as her plate was empty, she carried it to the sink and cleared the table of all but her husband's dishes. Leftovers stowed in the fridge and the dishwasher loaded, she lifted Eve from the swing, seat and all. "Good night."

He still didn't respond, giving her no choice but to retreat to the master bedroom and be thankful the ache in her heart wasn't fatal.

CHAPTER TWENTY

THE BEDROOM DOOR CLICKED SHUT AND ELI PUSHED AWAY HIS PLATE to make room for his arms and his head on the table. Beatrix had given him multiple opportunities to tell her about his surprise, but he'd frozen.

Why hadn't he told her everything? That he'd set the dining room table with candles and wine glasses to set a romantic mood? That he'd written a poem for her as a prelude to asking her to marry him again? That he loved her?

Now she was mad at him, probably every bit as much as the night they'd met.

He flattened his hands against the polished wood to keep from picking at the skin on his fingers. The cool surface only partially distracted him. Every mistake he'd made in the twelve days since their first meeting filtered through his mind. He'd screwed up more times in their short relationship than he had in the two months with his lone girlfriend in grad school.

His dad had it all wrong. Being so naïve that women took advantage wasn't the problem. Not knowing how to navigate the social world of normal people had caused the failures. He wasn't normal, and nothing could ever change it.

At least he was fairly certain Beatrix wouldn't divorce him. No matter the state of their marriage, she would never abandon their daughter. She loved Eve and Eve loved her.

More than an hour passed before he finally finished the kitchen cleanup and retrieved his laptop from the office next to his old bedroom, the one he'd slept in before Chloe had been admitted to the hospital. His whole life had changed since the day he'd moved in with his cousin. Not all of it had been bad, but very little had been easy. Being in love was no exception.

He trudged toward the living room, resigned to grading papers until he couldn't keep his eyes open. That sounded like a better option than having his wife lie with her back to him in bed, especially when she hadn't slept with him since Tuesday night.

Headlights flashed through the curtains in the dining room as he passed, highlighting the shadowy outlines of the bouquet and the other paraphernalia Morley Dash had said he needed. He hesitated for a moment before entering the room and turning the dimmer for the chandelier until the shadows disappeared.

The poem still lay beside the vase, with the jeweler's box on top of it. Ice shifted in the polished silver pail near the edge of the table, making the bottle of sparkling cider sink deeper into the bucket. Everything had been frozen in time, much like the connection between his brain and his mouth during supper.

He set the computer at his place setting and flopped into the chair. "I love you."

The words he'd practiced all afternoon escaped with no effort at all with no witnesses.

He opened his laptop and clicked through to the first essay. "I love you."

A gusty sigh made the petals of the closest flower quiver.

He read and reread the first sentence, unable to focus on the assignment. "I love you. I. Love. You. I love you. I feel it. Why can't I say it to her?"

A sniffle drew his attention to the arched doorway. Beatrix clutched a pile of clothes to her chest and brushed her fingers across her cheek.

"I came out to tell you I was sorry for making you uncomfortable and that I'd sleep in the spare room so you didn't feel like… This is what you couldn't tell me?"

Had she heard him practicing again?

He nodded, afraid to risk another bout of frozen brain.

She stepped into the room and approached the opposite side of the table. "A tablecloth and flowers and candles. I ruined your plans. First with pizza and then by insisting we eat in the kitchen. You wanted everything to be perfect. It *was* perfect until I took over."

Forcing his hand into motion, he handed her the paper. The velvet box flipped upside down, the sound muffled on the white cloth. "I should've told you. I wrote a poem for you."

"We both could've done better." Still standing, she set her armful on the table and took his offering. Her gaze lowered toward the contents. After an eternity of silence, she cleared her throat. "The moment I saw you, my heart knew. My hopes flew, but my brain said slow down. The first time I kissed you, my soul knew. My heart grew, though great loss made me drown. Through vows I spoke with you, my brain knew. The wind blew, chasing away my frown. Day after day with you, life anew. Love is true, only with you around."

He held his breath, hoping the words spoke to her the way he meant them.

The paper fluttered onto the silverware and came to rest against the stem of her wineglass. She flipped open the box as she picked it up. "It's beautiful. The poem too. I don't know what to say."

"The stones are tourmaline. Eve's birthstone and the month we got married. It's an engagement ring since we didn't go through the usual dating rituals." He rounded the table, determined to get the most important part right this time. Then he knelt at her feet and grasped her hand to slide the ring into place. "I love you, Beatrix. Will you marry me again? In a real wedding? With family and all the fancy clothes and a reception if you want it. I won't ever be perfect, but I want you to be happy that we got married."

"I'm not perfect, either." She dropped to her knees and flung her arms around him, hugging him tighter than she had the night of Chloe's death. "Yes, I'll marry you again, but only if we plan it together. I love you so much, and I'm happiest when we remember we can count on each other through whatever happens."

The feel of her body against his reminded him they hadn't made love for days—something he needed to remedy. He closed his eyes and pressed his lips to her neck, reveling in her familiar scent. "I've missed holding you when—"

A faint cry was immediately followed by a more insistent one.

Beatrix laughed softly in his ear. "We're not very good at scheduling our make-out sessions around Eve's meals yet. Want to cuddle with us on the couch while she nurses?"

"And then we can go to bed?"

"Absolutely." She kissed his jaw. "If you get Eve, I'll pour the bubbly cider. We can toast our engagement."

"I'd like that." The ring glinted in the light from the chandelier as he rose with her. "I'll meet you in the living room after I change her diaper."

Her smile made his stomach quiver, much like the first time they'd met. "I'm glad we're doing this together. One step at a time."

He leaned in for a quick kiss on his wife's lips. "Me too."

I HOPE YOU ENJOYED BEATRIX AND ELIJAH'S STORY AND WILL SHARE your thoughts in a review! You'll see more of their happily imperfect family in the other books of the Nerd Love series.

ABOUT THE AUTHOR

Mellanie Szereto is the *USA Today* Bestselling Author of over fifty romcoms and contemporary romances, most with characters who have plenty of life experience like herself. Whether you call them older, seasoned, mature, experienced, or later-in-life protagonists, they deserve love too! Her stories are often set in small towns with quirky main characters, fun secondary casts, and lots of humor. She enjoys gardening, cooking, and baking—as well as hiking to work off the fruits of her labor—and incorporates food into all of her stories. She lives in an old farmhouse in rural Indiana with her husband of thirty-seven years.

Visit her website for more information about her books!

www.ingramcontent.com/pod-product-compliance
Lightning Source LLC
LaVergne TN
LVHW020046110826
845155LV00029B/651

* 9 7 8 1 9 4 2 5 2 2 6 0 7 *